the Devil's DEMISE

CAVALERI BROTHERS #5

LILIAN HARRIS

This is a work of fiction. Names, characters, organizations, places, events, and incidences are either products of the author's imagination or used fictitiously.

© 2022 by Lilian Harris. All rights reserved.

No part of this book may be reproduced, or stored in a retrieval system, or transmitted in any form or by any means, electronic, mechanical, photocopying, recording, or otherwise, without the express written permission of the publisher.

Editor: Ms. K Edits

Interior Formatting: CPR Editing

Proofreader: Judy's Proofreading

Cover Design: Covers by Jules

Find your joy. Chase that rainbow.
And never give up trying.

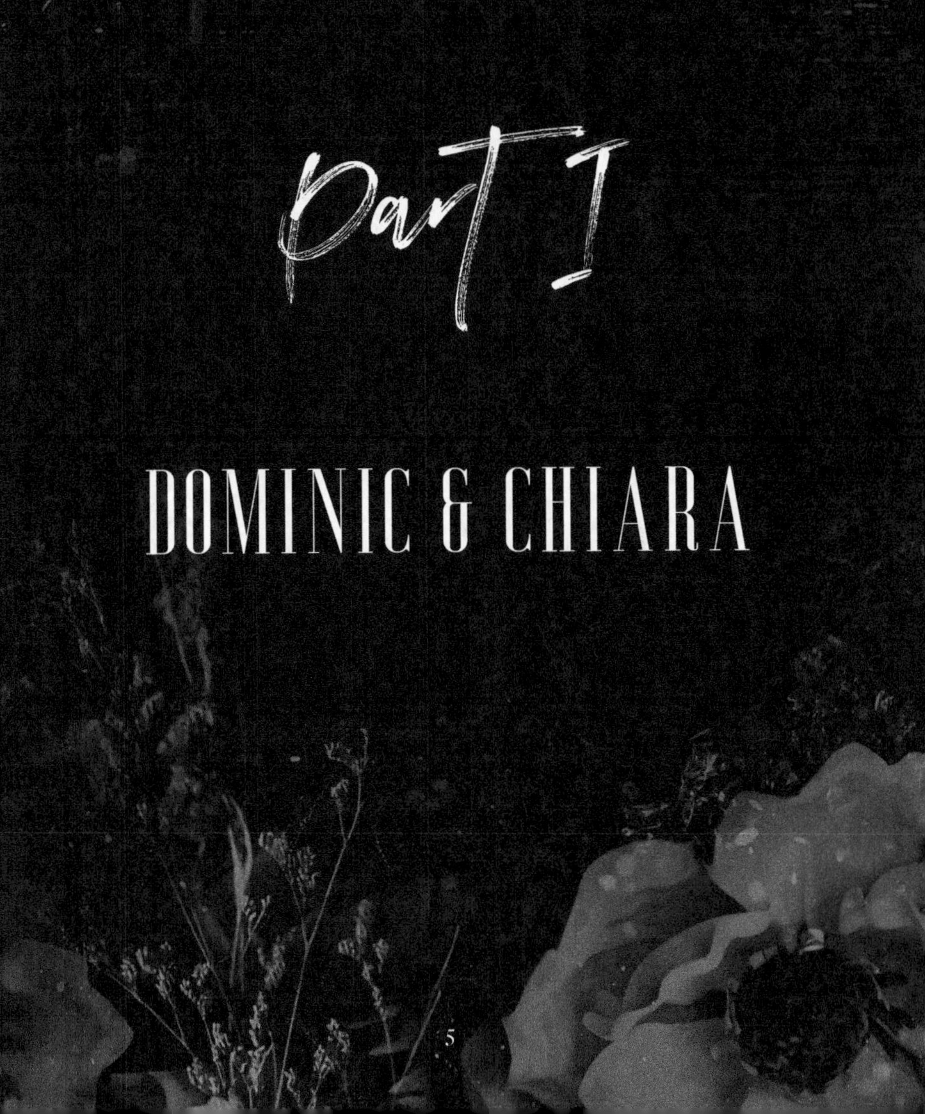

Part I
DOMINIC & CHIARA

CHIARA
FIVE AND A HALF YEARS LATER

"**A**re you here alone?" a man asks from behind me, his voice crackling in between the exploding music.

I twirl my red straw around in my virgin strawberry daiquiri, crossing one leg over the other. My thigh-high boots tug around my knees as I lift my drink and take a sip, completely ignoring him.

"You look too good to be drinking all by yourself." His lips are dangerously close to the curve of my ear, and the timbre of his tone is smooth, yet deep. Just what I like in a man. "How about I join you?"

Without waiting for a reply, he takes one of the swivel stools beside me, waving over the bartender and ordering a whiskey neat.

I continue to ignore him, my gaze transfixed on the mirror above the bar ahead. His eyes capture mine through it, and something in me catches on fire—that familiar knotting in my gut, the tensing and throbbing of my core.

My tongue takes a leisurely swipe of my lower lip as I hold his attention, and he doesn't dare waver.

His hand slides across the bar, all the way to mine, his fingers brushing over the top of it.

"A ring, huh?" he drawls, looking right at the side of my face as he swipes across my glistening six-carat diamond.

"That's right." My response is cool, indifference slinking between each word, the complete opposite of the desire swirling within me.

"And where's this husband of yours?" A crooked smirk captures the corner of his mouth as he faces me.

I can make out the hunger beating within him through the mirror. His fingertips graze the top of my hand, just enough to send tingles shooting down my body. This shouldn't turn me on as much as it does, yet here we are, and I'm enjoying the fuck out of it.

"He's off running his businesses." I don't dare look right at him. It'd be too much, too intense. "He's quite the busy man."

"What kind of husband leaves a pretty thing like yourself all alone? Especially at a place like this?"

It's then that my eyes flick to meet his, unable to stop from glancing at the face of this quite attractive man. I'm not at all ashamed to admit my gaze wanders down his dark blue button-down, admiring the material showcasing the thick ripples of the muscular form he conceals underneath.

Even in the dim lighting, I can easily make out the hills of his large biceps and his toned shoulders. I try not to stare, but my eyes are suddenly drifting down his chest and to the abs hiding beneath.

Another devilish smirk lines his sinful mouth, and I pull in a deep breath, attempting to quiet the vicious way I want him.

Would he take me bent over this bar for all to see?

A shuddered exhale escapes my heavy lungs. Immediately grasping my drink, I drown in a long, cold sip, needing it after that visual.

His eyes scan over the top of my hot-pink strappy shirt that my tits are nearly spilling out of. When his gaze tiptoes back to my face, I pop a brow, my lips curling with a tiniest of smiles.

"Like what you see?"

"Very much." His chest expands as he drags a heaving breath, those eyes pinned to mine. "Your husband is a lucky bastard."

My toes curl within my high heels and my core clenches, wanting what I shouldn't.

Needing it.

My attention returns to the mirror as I pick up my drink, downing almost the entire thing and practically slamming it back on the counter once I'm done.

"So, what brings you to a place like this?" He throws another question at me.

"You mean a gentleman's club?" I flash him a grin.

He nods once.

"Well, seeing as I own it . . . ." I swivel around to him. "It'd be strange for me not to be here." I lean into my seat. "I'm here almost every day. Question is, where have *you* been?"

"I guess fate brought me to the right place at the right time." He props a hand between my thighs, pulling my chair closer to his.

My breath stills in my chest, warmth permeating my pores

while he drags me nearer.

"Lucky you," I manage, and our connection only intensifies.

His jaw strains as his gaze swings down to admire my lips. "You bet your ass I am."

He gives my mouth a long, hot stare, and I badly want to show him just what my mouth can do when I'm on my knees.

"So, are you having a good time around all these beautiful women?" My fingers flitter across my chest, not in a way meant to flirt, but from the nerves beating across my prickly skin.

His gaze fastens to mine. "I certainly am. And *she's* quite beautiful."

My heart lurches as my stomach flips. How does he do that?

"Flattery will get you everywhere." I keep my tone casual, not wanting him to know how much this is affecting me, though he probably does.

"Is that so?" He leans over, that lustful mouth brushing against the shell of my ear. "Because I'm quite good at it."

I grab his shoulder, my nails biting into the hard flesh.

"What else are you good at?" I tease with my slinky tone.

Smoothly, he draws away, climbing off his seat and coming to stand in between my legs as he spins my chair around in one quick motion until I face outward. His palms come to rest on the bar behind me, caging me in within the steely frame of his towering body. He bends to the crook of my neck, his warm breath skittering over my flesh, my nipples tightening.

"Fuck," I mutter low.

But I know he's heard. I know he can sense my body's weakness for him.

"Dance with me and find out," he rasps into my ear, and the rumbly pitch of his voice pebbles my nipples.

"This isn't really the type of place people dance in." I can barely say that without panting. "Unless you're naked and onstage."

"Oh, baby . . ." His large palm envelops my hip, the fingers of his other hand dipping into the inside of my inner thigh. "That's not the kind of dancing I was talking about."

For a mere moment, I hesitate. I can't possibly do this. I can't go with someone who isn't my husband. I know what he wants from me. Dom would punish the hell out of me if another man dared to touch me.

I rise off the chair as he moves a step back, giving me his hand.

My free one creeps up his arm, and his muscles flex under my touch, our eyes boring into the other's as I tighten my grasp.

"Did I mention my office is soundproof?"

He chuckles, low and deep. Suddenly, something savage flashes in his eyes and he grasps my jaw in the span of his wide hand, bending his mouth into mine.

"I'll enjoy testing out its limits."

I go breathless, my inhales filled with gasps even as he pulls me out of my daze with the drag of his hand.

He leads me out into a long corridor, the subtle melody of the music now so light, we can hear our own breathing.

"I don't know if I should be doing this." I exhale a shabby breath, causing him to stop, to turn, to yank me until I smash into his solid body.

Both hands fist my hair, roughing through it, his lips hovering over mine. "But you want to, don't you? You like being bad."

His knee pushes into my pussy, and without feeling any shame, I ride him, the wave of pleasure growing the deeper he drives into me.

"Say it," he demands, tugging at my strands. "Tell me you want this. Tell me how bad you want my cock inside your tight little hole."

When all I do is groan, he removes his knee.

"Damn it. Don't stop," I bite back.

He yanks my head back, those heavy-lidded eyes greeting me, the storm within them brewing. "Then say it. I want to hear how bad you want to fuck me behind your husband's back."

"Y-yes . . ." I groan, needy and desperate.

He throws me up against the wall, forcing his hard body into mine, molding us perfectly as though somehow this is right. He drops one of his hands, roughly undoing the button of my jeans and practically ripping the zipper down.

"Are you wet, sweetheart? Is this pussy dripping for something new?"

"Yes. Oh, God," I whisper-cry when his fingers dip in past the zipper, flirting inches away from where I desperately need them. "Please . . ."

My hips arch, trying to take what he's denying me.

His deep-chested chuckle sends a quiver down to my core.

"Use your words." He drops his hand from my hair, now clutching my jaw within it.

Did I mention large, manly hands like his are my kryptonite?

"Please what?" His mouth lowers, perched close, our breaths tangled in heated desire.

"Please fuck me. Touch me however you want."

In a mere blink, his entire palm slips inside and cups my pussy. I can feel how soaked I am as he easily glides his hand up and down.

"Yes . . ." My lips part on a moan, and my eyes want to close, but I keep them open, wanting to look at him as he touches me.

"No panties, huh? You're a very bad girl, aren't you?"

"Always," is all I can manage when two fingers replace his palm, stroking both sides of my throbbing clit.

A jolt zaps into my back, my gut. I don't even know where exactly, but I feel everything at the same time, like I'm wired.

"Fuck!" My whispery shout lands around his jaw as he growls in approval, working his fingers faster.

"What would your husband say if he caught us? My hand taking what's his. What you're easily giving me, like my personal plaything."

"He'd kill you," I confidently manage through the gritting of my teeth.

And it's true. If another man were to touch me, Dom would break him in half before shooting his dick off.

"He can try," the man says, removing his fingers from me and dragging my jeans down.

"What are you . . . ?" My eyes pop wide, my pussy aching for him to finish.

Aligning our gazes, he continues to undress me until my pants are around my knees. All I do is grow hotter all over, circling my ass against the wall, needing him to release me from this torturous state.

"Turn around," he demands. "Palms against the wall and spread those thighs."

My chest trembles with scattered breaths, my brows bending in shameless pleasure.

"Now."

"Here?" I question, though still doing as I'm told, looking at him from over my shoulder.

"Here."

He presses into me, wrapping a hand around my throat, clutching it tight, while his fingers return to my clit, stroking slowly. A series of moans barrage out of me.

"Wish your husband could see how desperate you are for my

cock. My good little slut." His hand narrows around my neck, and I'm barely able to drag in air. "Let's see how good you can take it."

He thrusts three fingers inside me so hard I suffocate on a scream I can barely make. He curls those fingers, roughly slamming against my G-spot. My walls clench while his other hand cinches tighter around my throat.

"You like being used like my personal whore, don't you? Being spread open for anyone to see."

"Yes . . ." I gasp. "Don't stop, I'm—I'm almost there."

So close, I can almost taste it.

"Do you get this wet for your husband?" His tongue licks a path up to my ear, sucking my lobe into his hot mouth.

"No," I groan. "He usually leaves me to take care of myself. Too busy to satisfy me."

"That's a damn shame." His teeth scrape along the shell of my ear, his strokes getting harsher, making my body practically explode.

"Yes, fuck!" I cry, as his thumb rubs circles on my clit until my legs quiver, and that's all it takes. "Oh, God, yes!"

My scream echoes through the hall as he gives me everything, milking every tremor, working me until my body stills.

"You're incredible," he whispers, his lips meeting my nape as he leaves urgent kisses behind, even with his hand still wrapped around my throat.

"That was . . . hot." I exhale with exhaustion.

"I'm not done with you yet." He reaches for the door handle that leads into my office and pushes it open, taking my hand and leading me inside.

When I told Dom I wanted to run my own strip club, he didn't hesitate in his support. He funded the business once I found the perfect location, and Club Azalea was born. This time, I run it the right way. Nothing dirty happens here, not like it did at my father's place. I protect my girls.

The man's hands are on my hips as he kicks the door closed, leaving it unlocked. He tips my chin up with a finger, those eyes boring into me so hungrily, I can feel him . . . or more like sense him in the marrow of my bones. We're attuned, and it's scary and thrilling all at once.

He drops to the floor, looking up at me as he takes one of my feet, slowly lowering the zipper around my boot before removing it, then moving on to the other.

The tip of his tongue darts out as his gaze meets my pussy, and then he's removing my jeans completely before climbing back up my body. With a palm, he pushes me backward until the backs of my thighs hit the desk.

His hand curls around my throat, his thumb roughly brushing over my mouth before he pushes me down onto the desk, spreading my legs apart in one rough move.

"Such a pretty pussy," he groans, his thumbs massaging my wet lips, almost meeting my clit.

"Shit, I . . ."

"Need to come again, don't you?" he growls, gently gliding two fingers up my center, rousing my need so expertly I almost fly off the desk.

He plays me, his eyes on mine, devouring the raging of my breaths and the desire perched within my gaze. He devours it all, like a man starved. Gluttonous.

"Fuck me, please." I attempt to prop myself on my elbows, but he pushes me back down with a heavy palm, one finger barely entering me while a thumb brushes over my achy clit.

I groan in frustration as he massages me with the heel of his palm. God, the things his hands can do. I can't believe I'm even doing something like this. I never would've thought I would.

Since being married to Dom for four and a half years, I've never once thought about fucking a complete stranger. But I must admit, this is insanely hot, being naked in front of someone else, having him do all the dirty things to me.

I stare at the ceiling, my eyes rolling to the back of my head when his thick, heavy tongue swipes me from ass to clit.

"Yes! Fuck!" My nails scrape along the wood of my desk.

And just like that, he stops. I quickly jump to a seated position, frustration embedded in my gaze.

I find his hands on his black trousers, unbuttoning them, and his eyes perched to mine. The sound of the zipper dragging sends a shiver down my spine.

"Finally," I groan.

A smile crawls to my mouth as I reach for his powerful wrist, pulling him to me, and he lets me take control. My hands replace his as I hurriedly draw his pants and boxers down, my long fingers curling over his thick, hard cock.

"This is mine," I moan.

My pussy's dripping on my desk, and I rub myself on it as I stroke him. I slide off, crouching down and peering up at him as I swirl my tongue around the head of his length.

"Oh, fuck, baby," he groans, his hand on the back of my head, pushing me down his cock until I gag, my eyes watering over deliciously. "I like you full of me."

His hoarse and throaty voice has me burning for him, needing to feel this beautiful man inside me. He jerks against my tongue as I bob my head, not leaving an inch of him without the feel of my warmth.

He clutches my hair, dragging me back.

"I need to come inside you," he grits as my tongue runs circles over the tip of his cock. "Filthy little thing."

He yanks harder, pulling me upright before his mouth devours me, his tongue roughly parting my lips, entering inside, winding with mine.

He palms my ass, squeezing once before he's forcing my body down until I'm lying over the desk with him in between my thighs. My hands are on his back, his muscles stretching and flexing while I attempt to yank the button-down shirt up so I can feel his skin on mine.

He pitches back, his fingers on his tie as he slowly undoes it, and then he's working the buttons of his shirt, practically ripping them off. He removes the tie from around his thick neck while my fingers drift down my stomach, slipping inside me as I watch him take the shirt off. He eyes me hard on a guttural groan, cursing under his breath while I bite into my bottom lip.

Slipping the tie off, he balls it in his fist, using his other hand to yank my shirt down, freeing my breasts. He continues to watch me touch myself, his cock jerking as I moan and roll my hips.

He reaches for my pussy, pushing my hand away and rubbing his tie in between my soaked lips. With a devilish grin, I grab it from him, lining it in between my legs as I close them, stroking myself on the soft silk, my gasping growing louder the more he watches. It's exciting being watched, knowing it's turning him on.

"Fuck!" he roars before he jerks the tie from my grasp, and in a mere blink, he stuffs it into my mouth. "You taste good, don't you, baby?"

I nod, throwing my head back as his cock lines up with my entrance. His hands are on my ankles, and he pulls them apart, yanking me to him until my ass is hanging off the desk.

"Yeah, that's right, you do. Such a filthy slut, rubbing her sweet pussy on my tie."

I whimper as he pushes just an inch of himself inside me, and I try like mad to get him to fuck me, working my hips just so, but he doesn't give it to me.

"Please, Dom," I beg, forgetting this game we're playing.

"Oh, I'm Dom now, huh?" His wanton gaze runs down my body, his smirk doing all kinds of dirty things to me.

"You're always Dom to me, no matter how many different people we pretend to be. You're always mine."

His jaw tics with a possessive growl.

With my palms, I squeeze my large tits together, rolling my hardened nipples in between two fingers, knowing how crazy it makes him.

"Shit . . ." he groans, and I do it again.

He's on me in a flash, my throat at his mercy as he wraps his large hand around it, squeezing so hard I almost come. With a lustful look in his eyes, he thrusts his cock fully inside me with one hard motion, giving me every inch I desperately crave.

"Dom!" I tremble out a cry.

He pounds into me with ruthless strokes, his palm suddenly on the back of my neck, his forehead bowing against mine as our lips hover, tasting, owning each other's heavy breaths.

"You feel so good," I pant, my tongue snaking out to stroke his mouth, and he hisses once before he captures it, sucking, kissing me hungrily, so frantically, I almost come undone just from the sheer feeling of it.

His love, his devotion . . . it pours from everything he does. Everything he says. He knows just what I need, whether it's in the bedroom or outside of it. He somehow knows me even better than I know myself. And that says a lot because I know myself pretty damn well.

When we got married in a beautiful, simple city hall ceremony,

I never expected our life to be so good. Before we reunited, I thought I'd be alone, especially after I refused to marry Michael Marino, the son of the don of the Messina crime family. But I'd never let my father control me that way.

Though I never admitted it out loud back then, I wanted someone. I wanted the kind of love I'd read about in the books I'd spend hours digesting.

And Dom? He gave me that and so much more. My childhood best friend became my lover, my husband, and I never thought we'd get that far after I lost him when we were thirteen.

"Harder!" I beg.

My voice is needy, my lips brushing his, my toes curling as my body scorches up like flames have set it on fire.

"Yes, just like that . . . oh fu—" I stammer when his thumb rubs circles around my clit, making my walls clasp around him while his gaze holds mine.

Whenever he looks at me when we're tangled in madness together, it makes our connection that much more tangible, that much more profound. Because with him, it's not just sex. It's something magical.

"That's it, baby. Take that cock. Remember who you belong to." His voice is fierce, spearing me with urgency, and I feel it— the need to unravel.

His fingers spear through my hair, his cock growing harder, until with another powerful thrust, we crash and burn into the fire together.

His heavy chest falls over me, sweat peppering his skin, now slick against mine.

"Next time . . ." I pant. "You're a mechanic, and I'm a girl stuck on the side of the road with a flat."

This will definitely not be the last time we try this. Wow.

"Do I end up fixing your tire?" He breathes heavily, his heart racing against my own.

"Yeah." I grin. "Then you fuck me in the back of your car, because obviously I have no money to pay you with."

"Obviously." He chuckles, throaty and raspy. "Only if you're in a pair of tiny-ass jean shorts."

He squeezes my hip possessively, and I swear my pussy quivers.

"That can be arranged."

"Shit, Chiara. I'm getting hard again just thinking about it."

"Mmm," I purr against his neck, my long nails riding up his spine.

He bows his hips into me, and I hiss.

"So damn sensitive since you got pregnant. Always so willing to fuck."

"Oh, you have no idea."

My hands are on his ass, loving how hard it feels within my touch. He rears back away a fraction, arching a brow.

"I think I do if we count the amount of times your mouth woke me up in the middle of the night." A lazy smirk falls over his lips.

"Don't pretend you didn't like it." I narrow a playful gaze.

"Oh, I loved it, baby." His palm falls to my face, cradling my cheek. "Your dirty mouth sucking me dry while you touch your wet pussy, waiting for me to stretch it out . . ." His thumb brazenly brushes over my lips. "What's not to love?"

"We should probably get dressed and head home. We have the party tomorrow." The great thing about owning my own club is I get to have managers and I don't have to stay until closing.

"Okay." His voice goes sultry and deep-toned, making my insides shiver. He kisses in between my breasts before tucking his forearm under his chin and gazing up. "Did I tell you I love you today?"

I let out a soft laugh, my cheeks warming.

He gasps. "Did my Chiara just blush?"

"Shut up." I roll my eyes, swatting his hard, muscular shoulder. "I so did not."

"*Riiiight*. I won't tell anyone." He rises off me and starts to get dressed. "Wouldn't want the people here thinking you're going soft on them." He winks as he tucks his heavy length back into his pants. "Hey. My eyes are up here, gorgeous."

I shrug, all doe-eyed. "I'm sorry, sir. It's just that my husband has such a small penis. I'm not used to seeing one that big."

"Small, huh?" He shakes his head, a smirk snaking up his mouth until he's suddenly on me, flipping me over his shoulder, his palm smacking my ass as I giggle freely. "I'll show you small."

Two

DOMINIC

Waking up beside Chiara is my favorite thing. It feels like I've waited a whole lifetime to call her my wife.

Chiara Cavaleri. That's who she was always meant to be. And sure, the years between us were filled with hurt and misunderstandings, but still, we made it, no matter the walls that were so expertly keeping us apart.

She groans, tucked into my chest, where she most often likes to sleep. Chiara isn't the type of woman to need anyone, and the fact that she needs me . . . damn, it makes me feel like I'm the luckiest son of a bitch that ever walked the earth.

"What time is it?" she asks, a lazy smile on her face, her eyes still half-closed.

"Early, baby." I palm her ass, pressing her tighter against me. "Go back to sleep."

She groans, burrowing into my bicep, and my cock throbs at the sight of her.

"You're so warm . . ." She yawns again. "And cozy . . ." She throws a leg over my hip. "But I should probably get up."

"No, you shouldn't, baby. You're three months pregnant. It's okay to rest sometimes. In fact . . ." I slant my lips over hers, stroking them with mine. "It's mandatory."

With one arm tucked under her, I use my other to pull her closer.

She groans as I kiss her. "But I have so much to do."

"Not this early, you don't."

Another kiss against her jaw has her throwing her head back on a long, throaty moan, and my cock swells against her at the sound.

"The club is closed. The house is clean." My lips drift down her neck, marking her with my kisses, my teeth grazing her skin. "There's nothing to do but stay in bed with your husband."

"So damn tempting, because my husband is all sorts of hot." Her hand slips into my scalp, her pointy nails scratching me, and damn, it feels like heaven.

Our life so far has been everything either of us could've wanted. This slice of paradise we've created is everything that matters to me. My brothers and I, we finally got to live, every one of us, with the woman we love. The war is now a distant memory, and it's nice not to live that way anymore. We have each other. We're all family. The girls are close, too. A little too close, if you ask me, because if one of us messes up, they're all ganging up on the wrongdoer.

Tiptoes splatter outside our door, and we groan simultaneously.

"You think if we hide under the comforter, they won't see us?" she asks on a sweet laugh.

"Let's try it," I whisper, grabbing the blanket and quickly

enveloping us in it, just as the door opens.

Giggles fill the room as they come closer. Suddenly, two tiny people jump onto the bed with a monstrous growl.

"Oh, no!" I scream. "They found us! Run!"

Our three-and-a-half-year-old identical twin boys yank the comforter off our faces.

"I'm hungry!" Frankie pouts, sitting on my gut.

"Me too!" Gianni jumps on the edge of the bed, his hands in the air.

"Baby, stop that!" Chiara says. "You're gonna fall off and bust your head open."

He continues, and she blows out a sharp exhale.

"Come give your mama a squishy hug."

Her arms stretch out for him, and he comes running. He always does. She smiles as his chest lands on hers. Their thick black hair is just like their mother's, and their eyes, they're all mine.

They're like the perfect combo of both of us. Our family couldn't tell them apart for a while. The only obvious difference was the small birthmark on Frankie's hip.

But as they grew up, the differences were obvious. Gianni has quite the taste for destruction, while Frankie would rather build. Gianni loves to get dirty. He'd roll around in mud all day if we let him. But Frankie would scream if he even got a smudge on his face.

After Chiara got shot, the only bright spot was that she could still have children. The doctor told her she was very lucky with where the bullet hit, because an inch over, and our chances of having kids would've been gone.

We didn't plan the timing. We just let fate take the lead. When she got that positive pregnancy test, she cried. I did too. It was the rawest I've ever felt. Then it happened again, and man, it was like the first time.

I'll have as many kids with her as she'll let me. Little her-and-mes. I kind of hope this one is a girl, though. It'd be nice to have a little girl who's as tough as her mother is. We'll be finding out the gender today at our reveal party with the family, just in time for Matteo and Aida to come home from their time on Corvo Island.

They purchased a home there and spend the summers away on the beach like they once wanted. Over the years, their past has been on my mind. And that's only the parts they chose to share. I know there's more they won't talk about, and I understand why. It's theirs, that pain.

I've been there, closed up, refusing to let anyone in. But that all changed when we found Matteo, and then even more after Chiara and I got married and started a family of our own.

They say I'm different now. I laugh. I guess I didn't laugh a lot back then.

I tug Frankie against me, looking over at my beautiful wife. Her bare face is radiating with a glint in her eyes.

I love you, she mouths.

With a deep breath, I lower my lips to her forehead and kiss her because this is how I talk. This is my way of showing her what she means to me.

We stay like this for a while, holding onto the warmth, to our family, to the love always binding us together.

"Can we eat now?" Gianni pops his head up, his bright green eyes staring hard at me.

I swear, he's me. Hardheaded. Stubborn.

"Okay," I grumble, sitting up and flipping a laughing Frankie off my shoulder as Chiara grins. I reach for Gianni, who looks too comfortable against her, not that I blame him. "I've got him, baby."

"So overprotective." She grins, knowing I don't want her lifting heavy shit when she's carrying our baby.

"You know you love it when I get protective." I throw her a playful gaze, snatching up our other son and throwing a giggling Gianni over my other shoulder.

"Oh, I do, Mr. Cavaleri." Discreetly, her hand snakes to my ass, and she squeezes, her long nails dipping into my muscles. "I really do."

"Keep doing that, and I'm giving these kids to Sonia and you and me . . ." I jerk my head behind us. "We'll be back on that bed, and we won't be out of it for hours."

She bites her lower lip, her eyes lustful.

"Damn you, woman," I grunt.

"You can't go back to sleep!" Frankie chimes in as we start for the door.

Chiara laughs. "You two wear us out. We need it."

"You bet your ass we do. We're renting you two to Uncle Dante."

"What does renting mean?" Gianni asks.

Chiara and I only laugh harder, and once we make it downstairs, Sonia's humming from the kitchen grows nearer.

"I told you boys not to wake them." She shakes her head once we appear. "You two told me you were getting your trucks." A smile grips the outer edges of her mouth.

"Tricked ya." Gianni giggles, popping his head from my shoulder.

I swat him playfully on his behind.

"It's okay," Chiara says, giving her a hug before filling a mug with hot coffee and making one for me.

She takes a seat around the kitchen island while I drop both boys at the kitchen table.

"Morning, Sonia. Everything smells good."

"Of course. Now eat, everyone, while it's hot."

"Grab a plate for yourself," Chiara says. "Join us. You work too hard."

She's usually out the door, not wanting to encroach on our family time, but she fails to understand, no matter how many times we tell her, that she *is* family. She's been like a mom to us both, and like a grandma to our boys. I don't know what we'd do without her.

"You sure?" Her brows furrow.

"Yes." I plant a palm on her shoulder. "Please, sit. Let me serve you for once."

"You're a good boy." She pats my cheek before she clears her throat and takes a spot next to Chiara.

I go to work, getting everyone food.

"How are you feeling, dear?" she asks Chiara.

"Better. I think the nausea has finally ended."

"Oh, that's great news. You poor thing . . . all that sickness."

She shakes her head as I place her food before her—pancakes, bacon, and a croissant she made from scratch. She spoils us.

Chiara was sick to her stomach for weeks, unable to keep anything down, so much so that she was put on meds, which seem to be working well.

"Daddy, is Mommy having another boy?" Gianni asks. "I don't want a sister. She won't like cars or trucks."

"Yes, she will!" Frankie says. "I think it's a girl. What about you, Daddy?"

"I don't know, kid." I hand them their plates with chocolate chip pancakes. "But Mommy and I don't care. We will love him or her no matter what."

I look at her then, and she gazes at me with a tender smile. My heart is full, and it's a feeling I'll never get sick of.

Three

CHIARA

A little while later, while Sonia helps get the boys ready for the party, I stare at myself in the mirror while Dom is busy in the shower.

A red, skintight dress hits my knees, and the little baby bump is already making its appearance. I wonder if I'll have a daughter. If we'll have the kind of bond my mom and I once shared. Not to say I could never have it with my boys, but having a daughter . . . I don't know, it somehow would make me feel closer to my mom.

Being a mother is something I've always wanted. Having those boys gave me back something I had lost when I was shot. Something I was afraid I'd never get again. Every day before, I'd tried to convince myself I didn't care each time I didn't end up pregnant. I was afraid to hope. But even though it took time, I had my babies, and they're everything I could have ever wanted.

When I lost the first baby, when the doctor told me the dreadful news, I was numb, on the outside at least. But inside, I was someone else. Someone I didn't recognize. I had wanted that little baby so badly, and it had killed me to know my family had destroyed my chance of knowing that child. It took me a few months to truly mourn the loss, but the knowledge that I could have more . . . that's what saved me.

I recall the moment when the doctor came to see me after I woke from the surgery. I remember her white coat with that brown stain on her right sleeve, like she'd spilled coffee on it. I remember the way her thick brows bowed when she looked at me. And in that instant, I knew for certain. I wasn't a mother anymore.

The room spins as I stare at the bright lights appearing above. I'm fuzzy, like I'm shaking, yet I'm still, on a bed, in the hospital. I don't know how long I've been awake, but I haven't told a soul. I fear my world is about to crumble, and I want to stay on the side where it's still safe.

The water is everywhere, climbing up my nose. My lungs ache as I scream, drowning in the bright crimson, yet no sound comes out. I try to fight it, needing someone to get me out, to save my baby. But everything turns dark, and then I wake up here.

Maybe I'm not actually here. Maybe this is all some kind of messed-up dream. The baby is okay. I'm okay. Everything is okay.

I ball my shaky hand into a fist, and my nails sink into my palm until pain registers.

I have to be alive. Dead people don't feel pain. Right?

"You're awake!" Raquel's voice rips through my thoughts, and suddenly she's there with a gentle hand against my shoulder. "Are

you in pain? Do you need more meds?"

I shake my head with vigor, attempting to sit up. So I am alive. *But does that mean my baby is . . .*

"Hey, don't . . . Just lie down. You just had surgery."

"Su-surgery?" My mouth is parched, but I fight it. "What happened?"

I push myself up, ignoring the dizziness.

But you know what happened. You were shot.

"Is our baby . . ." I can't seem to finish the thought, a throb building behind my eyes.

Because I know. The baby . . . she's not here anymore. Tears fill my eyes, but I blink them away, biting down, fighting the treachery of my emotions.

No. You won't do this. You won't give up. She's still alive. She has to be.

Raquel's gaze widens for a mere second before she tightens her lips. "Let me get the doctor and call Dom. He just went to get us something to eat."

"Raq—"

But she's out the door before I finish.

No.

My chest rattles as breath after breath shoots out of me in a panic, tears starting to overshadow the hope I was trying so badly to hold on to.

The baby is dead, but I can't seem to cry. There's anger there too. It vibrates through me like a plague of my own damnation.

My father, he did this.

He killed my mother and my child. They're gone.

Because of him.

"Ahhh!" I scream, a fist slamming into the tray that sits directly over my bed.

The cup filled with water flips onto the blanket, ice-cold liquid hitting my thigh, but I don't even jump.

My ability to control my labored breathing is useless. My chest is closing in, and the room is somehow squeezing into me, caging me in.

I'm drowning. Again. My lungs burn. I claw at my throat, my breathing growing harsh.

No. I'm suffocating. The room spins, my gasping inhales fighting inside my lungs.

"Ms. Bianchi," the doctor calls, stepping inside.

I turn sharply to find Dom beside her.

"Don't call me by that name!" I roar. "Ever! Do you hear me?"

My body trembles as I register her. Through her black-rimmed glasses, she peers at me. The sympathy there . . . it clouds over her, and I fucking hate it.

"Just tell me!" I scream.

Dom sits next to me. His hand is on my knee, and I turn to him. I see it in his eyes—the aching, the bleeding. I shake my head.

"No. Don't fucking say it."

My emotions, they consume me. Everything hurts. I ache for that child, for the loss.

"Ms. . . . ah . . . Chiara. How are you feeling?"

"I feel like shit! Okay? Is everyone happy now?" My pitch rises, my exhales hammering through me. "Is my baby dead? Don't sugarcoat it. I know I was shot in my stomach. I remember when the bullet hit me and where. So tell me. Is she dead, Doc?"

"I'm so sorry, but the baby didn't—"

"Get out!" I yell louder.

The tears, they waver like a quiet storm until it hits like thunder. She stands there, tightening her thin lips.

"I said get out!" I point to the door. "Get the hell out of here!"

She finally nods, scurrying out.

"Baby, I'm sorr—"

"Don't do that! You knew. You should've been here to tell me as soon as I woke up! But you-you-you were gone," I sob, my control snapping.

The gaping wreckage of my heart . . . I can no longer hold on to it. I scream. I cry. I don't know for how long. But his arms come around me, and I no longer know why I was mad at him at all. Because in this moment, all I want is to hold on to him.

I swipe the tears from under my eyes, smudging some of my eyeliner, but I can't seem to care enough to fix it right now. All I want to do is hold on to this baby that's inside me and keep it safe.

The bathroom door swings open, and Dom is there with a towel wrapped around his hips, the deep V pointing to where I normally would crave him. But right now, all I can think about is how lucky we are to have what we have after everything that's been taken away.

"Hey, what's wrong?" he asks, concern fitting his face, his cheeks hollowing.

His bicep muscles strain as he uses a smaller towel to dry his hair, and he comes to stand behind me when I don't answer. I see him through the mirror, and a smile immediately forms on my face.

"Just thinking about how happy you make me."

"It's only getting better from here, baby." A hand twines around my stomach, his palm spreading across my lower abdomen. "I swear it."

"I hope so."

"Uncle Matteo and Aunt Aida are here!" the boys shout, jumping up and down.

The rest of us are gathered in the back, the yard set up with a long table, a white tablecloth draping it. Pink and blue plates and a balloon centerpiece are at the center. We catered some food, so no one had to cook, especially Sonia. We wanted her to have fun with us. And this time, we made sure the catering company was triple-vetted.

"What the hell?" Dante says. "I thought I was your favorite uncle."

"When Uncle Matteo's not here." Gianni giggles, his emerald eyes full of mischief. "He brings the best presents."

"Damn. It's like that?"

"Yeah," Matteo throws in, his footsteps getting closer. "It's like that."

Aida is all smiles beside him, both of them with huge bags in hand. Cecilia, their daughter, runs up to me, and I kneel so she can jump right into my arms. She's only two, and the cutest little thing with her big hazel eyes.

"Hey, pretty girl," I tell her, giving her a tender kiss on her cheek and rolling a hand down her long brown hair.

The boys jump all over Matteo like maniacs, and Matteo flips Frankie upside down while Gianni wraps his arms around his thigh.

"Aida." I go to her, embracing her in a tight hug. "I'm so happy you guys were able to cut your trip a little shorter. This means so much to us."

"We'd never miss it. We're both so happy for you." She pulls back just as Raquel comes out of the house, after having to use the ladies' room for the hundredth time.

Her hand rests on that round belly, where her son is quite

comfortable. Four-year-old Carnelia, her daughter, runs past her mother, her black hair twirling in the wind as she hops off to be with her cousins.

"Oh my God. There you are!" Raquel rushes over, but it's more like waddling. She's due any day now, so her running days have been numbered.

"How's little Tristen doing?" Aida asks as they hug.

She huffs. "Destroying my damn bladder. I swear he's trying to kill me in there." Her head shakes, her brows arching. "How he still has room to kick his mother all day, I don't know."

"Oh, yeah. I remember when Cecilia did the same. I could barely sleep those last few weeks. You're due in three days, right?"

"Yes, and I swear if this child is late, I'm pulling him out myself."

We all laugh, and then more people arrive. This time, it's Enzo and Jade, with Robby and Lauralyn with them. Their little girl is three and is Jade's replica down to her eyes.

I still can't believe Robby's twelve now. He's come a long way since the torture my family has put him through. In fact, Aida and Jade have put the past as far behind them as they can.

Jade has started a center for trafficked women, and with her guidance, that place has been a refuge for many women. It's thanks to her that Aida has gotten through her issues. She was one of the first people Jade helped. After the center opened, Aida continued to attend the meetings, and even assisted Jade with organizing events, and later on, began helping women at the center too.

"Hey, favorite uncle in the house!" Enzo calls, rolling up his sleeves as Jade walks up, embracing each of us.

Dante scoffs, getting off his seat and walking over to Enzo. "Sorry, bro. I've got news for you. Matteo here has been given that title."

Matteo shrugs, flipping his hands in the air, a huge smirk on his face as he hands all the kids presents that he and Aida brought from Portugal.

Lauralyn peers up at her father, batting her long lashes, a smile perched on her little mouth.

He jokingly huffs and rolls his eyes. "Go. Get your gift."

"Yay!" Lauralyn claps, running to Matteo and giving him a huge hug.

"This is war," Enzo calls to his brother. "And I play dirty." He rubs his palms, his gaze narrowing playfully.

"Bring it," Matteo throws back, his brows swinging up and down. "'Cause I do too."

Dom's shaking his head as he looks on to see what the kids are getting. There are dolls and cars and gadgets of all kinds.

"Did you guys buy the whole store?" I ask with laughter flitting my tone, loving that they enjoy spoiling our children.

"More or less." Matteo grins as the kids excitedly open everything.

"Okay, the very pregnant lady's gotta sit." Raquel shuffles on her feet.

Dante's suddenly beside her. "Shit. Come on, baby."

He curls an arm around her hip, leading her to one of the chairs as the ladies and I follow, and he helps her settle down.

"Thanks, babe," she tells him, gazing up at him with so much devotion in her eyes.

He lowers his mouth to her forehead and kisses her, his eyes falling shut as he inhales deeply. In this moment, I'm smiling, seeing how loved my cousin is.

It's funny sometimes, where one can start and where we can end up. Each of us has a story of how we met, lies and pain filling up the pages, but here we all are—happy, content . . . a good life.

He takes his spot next to her, picking up her hand and holding it on his lap. Her head immediately falls on his shoulder.

Jade and I decide to have a seat too, me next to my cousin, and her beside me. Once the kids are busy playing with their stuff, Matteo sits right by Aida, opposite us.

Her attention immediately goes to him, and he holds her gaze, his mouth tilting at the corner. In their silence, one can literally feel their love, and it's so beautiful. Out of all of us, they deserve it most of all.

I take a long breath, observing the people I love, laughing, their conversations buzzing while filling their plates.

"So . . ." Jade turns to me. "Any gut feelings?"

"Honestly? I think it's a girl, or maybe I kind of want it to be." I peer at each of them. "I mean, I want a healthy baby most of all, but a girl would be nice, ya know?"

"Of course. You're allowed to have a preference," Jade says, squeezing her hand on top of mine in reassurance.

"Most do." Raquel picks up her glass of water. "I definitely wanted a boy because I'm so done after this kid."

"That's what they all say." I give her a knowing look.

"No way." Her eyes grow large. "I'm not having any more after this one."

Dante's gaze wanders to her. "Never say never, sweetheart."

"Uh-uh." Lighthearted annoyance greets her features. "I'm gonna make you push it out next time."

"And that's when I exit this conversation." His face sets with a grimace as he slowly turns away.

"He'd have twenty kids," Raquel says. "The man is nuts."

"I heard that." He speaks low, not looking at us this time, but cracking a smirk.

She bumps her shoulder into him on a laugh. "Good. I wasn't

hiding it."

His chuckle is deep, and he snaps his attention back to us, a hand around her neck as he pulls her in to kiss her temple. "I love you. That's the only reason I'd be happy with as many as you'd be willing to have."

We all "aww" at them, while Raquel rolls her eyes with a groan, smiling ridiculously.

"Of course he has to say something as romantic as that."

He winks at us. "How else do you think I got to marry someone like you?"

"By tricking me?"

"Wow, Mrs. Cavaleri. You wound me." Both palms cling to his chest as he lets her go.

She throws her arms around his neck, kissing him slow.

"I'll make it up to you when we're home." Her voice grows low, while his eyes don't hide how he's feeling right about now.

"Get a damn room!" Enzo sticks a finger into his mouth, pretending to throw up, just as he and Dom tread over to us.

"Oh, you leave them alone," Sonia chides with a dismissive wave of her hand. Janet is beside her.

On days like this, all of us together, happy, it reminds me that my father didn't win. That we did. After everything they put us through, we made it to the top.

I hope that wherever they are, they can see us. And I hope it hurts like hell.

"You guys wanna play some ball?" Enzo asks his brothers, rubbing his palms together. "Two on two?"

"I've got Dom." Dante smirks, slapping his brother on the chest.

"That's all right." Matteo looks at Enzo. "We're younger and faster. We'll smoke you two."

"Fuck yeah, we will!" Enzo jumps to his feet.

"Language!" Jade widens her eyes, pivoting around in the patio seat, giving him a stern look from behind her shoulder.

"Sorry, baby," he whispers, pretending to zipper his mouth.

Swooping down, he cups her nape and kisses her softly against her lips.

"Who needs to get a room now?" Dante teases with a chuckle, getting Enzo to pull away before he punches Dante in the gut.

He keels over with a groan, pretending to be hurt. "I see what you're trying to do." He nods as he rights himself. "You're trying to get rid of your competition. Not gonna work."

"We'll see about that." Enzo scoffs.

Those guys are a competitive bunch.

"Good luck, boys," I say.

They all wave with smiles, heading for the basketball court on the other end of the yard.

We watch them disappear out of sight, and silence grows between us as we take in our children. Their laughter and yelps drift around us. Some jump on the large trampoline Dante had purchased for the twins on their third birthday, while others are playing on the swing and sandbox.

Janet and Sonia insisted on keeping an eye on them while we get some time to relax. Relaxing isn't something I'm comfortable with, though. I always feel the need to be on the go, to keep my mind occupied, or else I remember my life before.

"You guys ever think about . . . the past?" I'm the first to break with conversation.

"All the time." Aida sighs, her gaze frozen to mine, a furrow forming between her brows.

"Yeah." I nod. "Me too."

Jade picks up a glass of mimosa, sipping slowly before placing it back down on the side table beside her. "When did you all finally realize that it's okay to breathe again? That it's finally safe enough?"

I tilt my head at the question, narrowing my eyes as I think about the answer. Raquel and Aida do the same.

"I'll start," Jade continues, clearing her throat, her eyes distant. "For me, it was when Enzo adopted Robby. I felt this instant relief, like my life finally made sense. Like those men can't get us anymore because we're a real family now."

Her shoulders climb up from the long inhale she takes.

Aida runs a hand through her long, blonde hair, looking up to the clear blue sky for a moment before her eyes fall to each of us.

"It was when we first got to Corvo Island many months later." She exhales a heavy sigh. "I felt trapped for so long, in that house, with that man, always wondering, 'What's next. When will it all be over? When will I die? When will Matteo?'" She purses her lips in a faint smile. "But that island . . . it saved me. It gave me peace. It made me feel protected. I knew no one would get me there. I think that's why I didn't want to leave for a while. Until I knew that when I did, no one would hurt me on the other side."

There's a collective nod, and Raquel goes next, while I really consider my entire life and when that pivotal point took root.

"I think once I had Carnelia and realized I was nothing like my mother. For so long, I was afraid I'd become like her. That it was in my DNA, whether I liked it or not. But when I had her, and with each growing year, I knew that girl was my whole world and I'd die before I let her feel an ounce of what my mother made me endure."

When it's finally my turn, when they all look to me for my

answer, I say what I knew all along. That exact moment when that dark cloud overhead drifted away.

"The day the twins were born." My lips lift at the corners, my eyes going downcast. "Even when the doctor assured me I could have kids after I got shot, I didn't wanna believe it. Not really. I had this heaviness in my chest. Fear, I think. I held onto it, until they came out of me with a cry so loud, I welcomed it with tears. It was in that moment that I felt okay." I finally glance up again. "For once in my life, I had something my father couldn't take from me. And I know he'll never take anything again. From any of us."

"That's right." Jade picks up her drink and lifts it in the air.

We do the same, clanking our glasses together with happiness radiating through us, like a burst of light, shining over the once-cloudy skies.

I don't know how long we talk for, but before we know it, Sonia is bringing out a cake made of white fondant, decorated with yellow stars and a sleeping baby on top of it.

"It's time!" she announces, placing it on the dessert table for Dom and me to cut into.

My heartbeats pound like crazy as Janet goes off to tell the guys to end their game.

When they return minutes later, Dom reaches for my hand and squeezes it.

"You ready, baby girl?" His voice is warm and raspy against the space below my ear.

"I think so."

In this moment, I think about my mom. It seems like she's there with me at every big moment in my life. Every pregnancy, every birth, every time I'm sad or happy, I start to think of her as though she's standing right beside me.

Maybe she is. Maybe we just can't see those we love once they pass, even when they're right in front of us.

Taking a deep breath, I get to my feet, my hand still tucked in Dom's as we head toward the dessert table adorned with rustic flowers. Everyone gathers around us.

"I still got a shot at becoming the favorite uncle with this one," Enzo throws out.

"You wish," Matteo says on a chuckle, gathering Aida to his side, with Enzo and Jade beside them.

"Gianni. Frankie. Come on, boys," Dom calls. "We're going to find out if you two are having a brother or a sister."

They drop their cement trucks that Matteo and Aida got them and run to us, their toothy grins bright and full of youthful excitement.

"Who you got? Boy or girl?" Dante kneels, asking Frankie.

He twists his mouth around and looks up at me with a smile. "A girl."

"All right." Dante nods, his mouth quirking up, then turns to Gianni. "And you?"

"A brother." He crosses his tiny arms over his chest and lifts his chin in the air.

Dante rises with a laugh, ruffling Gianni's hair. "You're gonna love the baby no matter what."

"Only if she likes cars." He narrows a mean stare.

That gets us all laughing as I pick up the knife on the table, my pulse thundering wildly in my throat. My entire body vibrates with excitement.

Dom places his hands over mine, and my gaze wanders to my husband's, unsure how with each growing year I love him more. It's as though my heart grows to fit all this love I've been lucky to have.

As we place the knife against the cake, I think of my mother, who never got to see her child grow up, and I hope that I get to have that chance. That I can live to see my babies get older, to experience the kind of relationship I have with their father. Because everyone deserves that, to feel the epic kind of love. The kind that grows. The kind that doesn't wither your soul away, but helps it soar. And with Dom, I fly. I leap. And I know if I fall, he'll be there to catch me.

"I'm ready," I tell him with a deep breath.

With his nod, we drop the knife into the cake as slowly as possible, like we don't want this moment to end.

"It's pink!" Frankie yells from beside me. "It's pink!"

I gasp, staring at the first sight of the filling.

A girl. Oh my God.

My eyes water over, my throat clogging up with emotions as we drop the knife and look at one another.

"You're having a daughter," I cry as he holds my face in his hands, his gaze glazing over.

"And I hope she's every bit like her mother. Tough. Loving. A total badass."

"Dom . . ." I throw my arms around his shoulders as everyone whistles and cheers around us.

Athena Rose Cavaleri. That's what I'm going to name her, after my mom. A sudden chill rushes down my right arm, a feather-like touch skating over it.

When I look up at the cherry blossom tree behind Dom's back, the flowers sway, yet there's not a trace of wind at all.

Mom.

I grin, knowing it has to be her. I want to believe that so badly.

Once it sways again, my face brightens and my heart expands, because I know for certain she's been here, watching me after all.

Four

DOMINIC
TWENTY YEARS LATER - AGE 54

"It's a perfect day for a wedding. Wouldn't you say, Mrs. Cavaleri?" I leave a kiss on the back of her head, being careful not to ruin her hair, which is still as long as I first remember it on our wedding day.

She was and still is the most breathtaking woman I have ever laid my eyes on.

"Can you believe it?" She adds another coat of red lipstick in front of the full-length mirror. "How is this even possible? How's our baby old enough to get married?"

She puts the lipstick back in her sparkly black bag, matching the long black gown she's wearing.

Frankie is in the room next door with his groomsmen, while Chiara and I decided to sneak away and give ourselves a few minutes alone. It's a damn big day for us too. The little boy we remember, who ran around the house with his brother and sister, pretending to be a monster, is now a twenty-four-year-old man who's about to marry Savannah, a wonderful young woman he met in high school. They began dating when they were seniors, and both ended up at the same college.

He's working as an architect, and definitely is smarter than his old man, while she's going to become a vet. They couldn't be more perfect for one another.

I'm immensely proud of all my kids. Each of them is different, and each one of them is special to Chiara and me.

Gianni, though . . . he can't seem to get the whole relationship thing down. I say he just hasn't found the right one. But when he does, I know he'll love the hell out of her. Because under that tough exterior is a big heart.

I should know. I was a lot like him once upon a time.

For some of us, it just takes a little longer to find that special someone. My brothers and I are a good example of that.

Gianni decided to skip college. No matter how much his mother tried to talk him into it, he made up his mind. So instead, he's been working for me since he was a senior, in the hopes of one day taking over as CEO of our company when I'm too old to do it myself.

Athena, on the other hand, is working toward becoming a lawyer. I'm hoping I can convince her to work in-house for me and her uncles. We'll see, though. She's like her mother. When she wants something, no one can change her mind. Some might call that stubborn. I, on the other hand, call it determination. And my girls, they're that, all right.

Chiara straightens her dress, fixing the V-neck at the front and the thin straps sitting over her slender shoulders.

"Did I tell you how beautiful you look tonight?" I grip her hip with my hand, spinning her to me, and her chest lands hard against mine.

"You did." She brushes her thumb over my lips. "So many times."

I drag a long breath into my hollow lungs, my heart tightening as she bores those heavenly eyes into mine.

"You still manage to take my breath away," I tell her, cupping her face and gently kissing her jaw.

"And you, my handsome husband, still make my heart skip a beat."

"Aren't we damn lucky?" I loop my arms around the small of her back while hers fall over my shoulders.

Together, we sway, even though there's no melody to greet us. But with this love, there's always music somewhere.

"Thank you," I say, my palm clasping her nape, pulling her in for a kiss to the corner of her mouth.

"For what, baby?"

"For you," I breathe. "For this life you've given me. For the children we have. It's all because of you." Emotions settle in the back of my throat, and I find the same in the glistening of her eyes. "It's all thanks to that little girl who decided to be my friend, even while everyone else turned away. I owe everything to you, Chiara. You're the love of my life."

Her full lips wind up in that sexy way. "I think you had something to do with it too."

Goddamn, this woman is stunning.

"If you didn't have that shit on your lips right now . . ." I clench my jaw as my cock stirs to life. "I'd kiss the hell out of you, baby."

"Later, then?" She arches a single brow.

"Oh . . ." My hand slides down to her ass, squeezing it. "Definitely later, and a lot more than just that."

Her chest rises in the way it does when she's turned on.

There's a soft knock on the door as we continue to stare at one another.

"Come in," Chiara says as the door opens.

"Mom. Dad," Athena says as her heels clack inside. "What are you guys doing in here?"

"Hiding away with your mother, of course." I wink at Chiara before we both look at our beautiful daughter.

"Gross, Dad." She rolls her eyes, fighting a grin, and I swear I see Chiara.

Chiara's laughter fills the room as she turns to stand at my side, her arm wrapped around my lower back. "Would you prefer if I hated your father?"

"No." Athena walks up to us, jutting her chin. "But I'd rather avoid you both when you get all lovey and disgusting."

Her faint smile proves she's lying. She likes seeing us happy.

"You know, sweetheart . . ." I say. "When you're our age and have a good man by your side, you'll remember us this way."

She scoffs, planting a hand on her hip. "Men are idiots."

She pauses, her eyes widening for only a second before she disappears behind her anger.

"Sorry, Dad," she throws in when I pop my brows. "But it's true. Most of them are assholes. I'm never getting married because men like you just don't exist in my generation. I'm going to live alone and destroy every one of them in the courtroom."

"Wow," Chiara adds. "Seems like you have your whole life planned out."

"Don't look at me like that, Mom." She flips a hand through her long, jet-black hair, her green eyes zapping to her mother.

"Like what?" Chiara shrugs. "I'm just looking in a normal way."

Chiara's body rolls with a small laugh.

"Ah, no. You're looking at me in your 'mom' way. Like you think I'll change my mind. I know exactly what you're thinking. I absolutely will *not* change my mind."

Chiara places a hand on her shoulder. "Oh, my sweet baby. I'm sorry he broke your heart."

My daughter's eyes drop to the floor as Chiara continues.

"I just think one heartbreak doesn't mean you'll never find the one. That's all. Plus . . ." She lowers her hand. "Your father and I hated Tom anyway."

"What?" She gapes at both of us, her mouth parted.

"It's true." I nod. "There was something about him. Never liked that idiot."

"Why didn't you two say something?"

"Because you seemed happy, and we didn't exactly have a reason for our mistrust of him," Chiara says. "We were hoping that if we were right, he'd eventually show his true colors."

"Well, he definitely did when I caught him sleeping with my so-called best friend."

"I can kill him," I whisper. "The offer still stands."

And she has no idea how serious I actually am.

"Tempting. But I'll pass." She huffs. "He's not worth it. None of them are."

I fucking swear I want to find that boy and rip his goddamn throat out for hurting my baby.

When I found out what he did, when Athena was sobbing in her mother's arms, it took all three of my brothers to stop me from getting into my car and driving to that bastard's apartment. I would've ended him.

Our kids don't know anything about our past. My brothers and I have done a great job of keeping it secret, and we intend to keep it that way.

It's been three months since Athena's relationship with the asshole ended, and I know she's still hurting, no matter how strong she pretends to be. She loved him, and he broke her trust.

A loud knock prompts us all to turn toward the adjoining door with the groomsmen on the other side of it. When the door opens, Dante is there, a glass of whiskey in his hand.

"It's time, brother." He grins at me. "A final toast with the boys before we watch your boy get married?"

I grab my wife's hand, pulling it up to my mouth and leaving a kiss on the top of it. "Let's go."

She nods, the corner of her mouth curling up, and we all follow my brother out.

Chiara walks up to Frankie, clasping his face in her hands as she stares up at him. "I'm so proud of you."

"Thanks, Ma." He circles his arms around her and hugs her tight.

Dante clasps me on the back. "I can't believe he's getting married." He sighs deeply. "How the hell did we get old?"

"I don't even know."

"At least we're young enough to still get boners," Enzo adds, appearing beside Dante.

"Thank fuck for that." Dante chuckles.

"What are we thankful for?" Matteo walks up to us, a beer in his hand, his past no longer etched on his features like it once was.

"That we can still get hard for our wives."

His laugh is hearty as he shakes his head. "I'm just grateful I no longer have to take any of that advice from Enzo."

Enzo snickers playfully. "I taught you everything you know."

Frankie marches to us, playing with the cuffs of his suit jacket.

"Nervous, son?" I ask. "Because you don't have to be. Not when she's the right woman, and she is."

"Thanks, Dad." He inhales a quick breath. "I know she is."

His smile is wide and true as he says that.

Gianni comes toward us. "You sure you wanna do this?" He smirks, slapping a palm on his brother's back. "Because I'm tellin' you, the single life . . ." He quirks a brow. "That's where it's at."

I shoot him a glare, and he pushes his black hair out of his face.

"Sorry, Dad, but it's true. I like doing whatever the hell I want with whoever I want." His smirk deepens as he winks at an irritated Frankie.

"You know," Enzo tells him. "I once thought the same, and then I met your aunt Jade. My life has only gotten better."

Gianni merely waves a dismissive hand, but Enzo goes on anyway.

"When you love her, really love her, no other woman on earth will matter." He pins him with a deep look that speaks to his devotion to his wife. "I hope you find her one day, Gianni, because she's out there, waiting for you."

That gets my son's eyes to expand just a little.

"Look," I say to Frankie. "Life isn't without its problems. Everyone has them. It's what you do with them that matters. So as long as you two are always on each other's side, keeping the other together, you can make it through anything."

"Yeah, listen to your dad," Matteo says, swinging his arm around Frankie's back. "But whatever you do . . ." His voice lowers. " . . . don't ever take any advice from your uncle Enzo."

Laughter fills the room, and then it's time, really time to watch my boy tie his life to another. I can't wait for his life to truly begin.

Everyone exits toward the outdoor patio of the hotel we booked for the event. In the faint distance, the sound of the string quartet starts to play. Once we're closer, my brothers go and take their seats, while the maître d' steps up to line us up out in the hall. Chiara and I intend to walk our son down the aisle together.

The bridesmaids and groomsmen start heading out, and then it's our turn.

Hooking our arms through Frankie's, we give him a final look before the door pulls open.

As we proceed down the aisle with the eyes of all our friends and family on us, I'm reminded of the boy I once was, the hardship I've endured, never realizing what stood ahead for me.

For all of us.

Now that I know, I don't regret a single thing that led me to this moment.

Part II

DANTE & RAQUEL

RAQUEL

It's been a month since Matteo and Aida escaped the hell they've known for too long, and finally the chaos all of us have known is no more. I don't miss any of it. I don't even miss my mother, wherever she is.

I lay my head in Dante's lap while his fingers stroke up and down my arm as he stares down at me, his eyes filled with love.

I could practically feel it as though it's tangible. Mine.

The chill has just arrived in the city and Central Park isn't filled with people like it normally is in the spring. The area Dante took us to is even less populated. The Belvedere Castle is our backdrop, and I can't say I've ever been here. And what a shame that is, because it's beautiful here.

"I had the best day," I say, grabbing his wrist, my lips brushing his knuckles, kissing them.

"I'm glad, baby, but I have one more surprise for you." His mouth winds up at the corner and my stomach dips as I squeeze my thighs, arousal setting between them.

His jaw flexes, his eyes turning hooded. "Later." His tone turns seductive, that low, deep-chested growl setting me on fire. "Let's pack up." He lowers his face to mine, a hand around my throat, his thumb dipping deeper into my pulse as he kisses me. Hard.

I groan as his tongue languidly slides over mine. "Fuck, baby . . ." He strokes my lips with his. "If we don't go now, I'm gonna have to reach under those jeans, pull those panties to the side, and fill that pussy with my fingers."

"Oh my God," I moan as he backs away a fraction, those eyes practically tearing off my clothes. My heartbeats grow heavy, my chest releasing harsh gasps.

Would it be so bad? I mean, there aren't that many people here and we do have a blanket.

"Don't look at me that way," he grunts under his breath. "You know what that does to me." His inhales turn rough, his chest expanding, his fingers around my neck deepening.

He runs his other hand down his face, looking up to the sky for a moment before he pulls me up into his lap, his large hands around my hips as I settle over his lap.

"You drive me insane, sweetheart. The shit you do to me . . ." He exhales sharply, his nose leaning to my neck, running up and down. His lips meet my skin, showering me with soft kisses while my pulse thrashes wildly.

His heavy, hard cock rubs around my achy clit. All I want is to rock against it, but I fight it, remembering we aren't alone.

"I love you, Raquel. Only you." Another kiss, his teeth softly biting, his growl set with a dark edge as I squirm, needing him inside me. "We gotta go though, baby. Before I lose my mind with how badly I want to fuck you while everyone here watches what I can make your body do."

"Dante," I whisper on a moan.

He somehow makes it to his feet, my legs still wrapped around him. With another kiss to my lips, he slides me down his body, then packs up the empty hot chocolate cups and throws them into the basket filled with baked goods and chardonnay.

Hand in hand we stroll toward the castle. "Have you ever been inside?" he asks, his eyes darting to mine.

"No, never. But I heard it's beautiful."

"Nowhere as beautiful as you."

My cheeks flush as I peer down, squeezing his hand in mine. "You're not too bad to look at either."

Chuckling, he bumps me with his shoulder just as we climb up the first set of stairs. He warned me to wear comfortable shoes, so I'm in a pair of flat boots, and now I see why.

After we make it all the way to the third floor, entering the rooftop, all those steps are finally worth it, because that view . . . "Wow!" My fingers clasp the stony edge, gazing over onto the lake—green grass, trees just past the water, buildings towering in the distance. We're alone up here, which is kind of odd, considering how popular this place is.

"Wow is right," he breathes against my neck from behind, his palms tightening around my hips. Then they're gone, and I suddenly feel colder, needing them back around me.

I pivot toward him, intending to tell him just that but I don't get the chance. I slap a hand to my mouth, my eyes growing large as I take in the sight before me, my heart beating so fast, it will probably burst.

His smile is wide as he kneels before me on one knee, reaching into his pocket. As he does, music starts to play, and four people enter the rooftop. I immediately recognize the song. It's the one we danced to many times because it's my favorite. The beat from "Infinity" by Jaymes Young fills the space as tears spring to life within my eyes when a ring box appears in his hand.

Once he opens it, I'm overflowing with emotions, unable to hold them in. One thing Dante has said he regrets is never getting down on one knee to propose the right way, with a ring and all. But I didn't have any regrets in how our love story began. He came into my life when it was in ruins, when I thought I'd never get out of the forced marriage my parents arranged. I thought I'd die or suffer in agony with Carlito as my husband.

I never had imagined that I'd end up with someone as good to me as Dante is. But there he was, giving me a new life. A fresh start. He's been the one constant in my world from that day on. The one I can count on. So a ring was the last thing on my mind. I didn't need it. I just needed him.

He surprises me daily with his thoughtfulness, his affection. He's the type of man women dream about. But I didn't have to dream too long because he found me and made me his.

I don't care about the reasons. He was never a bad man, even when he lied. His love was pure even when his heart may not have been at the time he met me. But if it weren't for him, we'd never have what we do right now.

I hope wherever my mother is, she knows how happy I finally am, and that she didn't get to ruin my life for her benefit.

"Raquel." Dante smiles. "I never thought I'd ever end up finding someone like you. But you changed me, for the better, baby. And though we're married already, I needed to do it right, the way I should've from the start. So if you would agree to be my wife a second time, you'd make me the happiest man in the world."

"Ask me," I cry, swiping away the tears tracking down my cheeks. "Just ask me."

"Raquel Cavaleri, will you be my wife?" A smirk teases the rim of his lips. "Again?"

A blundering laugh escapes me as I sniffle, nodding. "Yes, I'll be your wife no matter how many times you ask."

"Good. Because I'd marry you over and over again." His grin is infectious as he slides the ring onto my finger, his eyes fastened to mine, just as tightly as his soul is bound to me for life.

When he gets to his feet, he lifts me into the air, and smashes his lips to my own for a kiss that'll last a lifetime.

Two

RAQUEL
FIVE MONTHS LATER

I stare down at the large, sparkling engagement ring he gave me five months ago, remembering that very day he proposed. My finger brushes over the firm edges of the round diamond and I breathe in a soft inhale, my eyes closed, the smell of freshly cut grass filling my senses like I'm back there again.

After he slipped the ring on my finger, he told me he wanted us to have an actual wedding with all our friends and family. He wanted us to have something we could look back on, something to show our children. And to be honest, I wanted that too. So, we decided on having a small wedding in our home.

Here we are on our wedding day, five months later. A shiver runs up my spine, knowing in a short while, I'll be walking down the aisle to him.

My husband.

The word still gives me butterflies.

"Damn, cuz," Chiara says from behind. "Your train is massive. You could hide a dead body under here."

She's not exactly kidding. It is pretty long. It was the first dress I tried on, and I knew, no matter how many I slipped into, it'd be the one. And in the end, it was.

It's a good thing I didn't leave that decision to Chiara because the one she liked for me . . . well, let's just say I wouldn't be caught dead in it.

"Come on, try it on." Chiara *holds a slinky white gown that cuts so low in the front, it would show my belly button.*

I pull back my lips in a grimace. "I'd never wear that," I whisper, looking around to make sure the saleswoman isn't around. Dante closed the store for me, and the ladies and I get to sip on champagne while I decide what dress to buy. There are a crap ton here—short, long. I mean, they have everything, and it's all crazy expensive. He told me not to concern myself with that and has instructed the saleswoman to put whatever I choose on his card. But I still don't want to take advantage just for one day.

"No one said you had to marry the dress." She rolls her eyes teasingly. "But try it on anyway. Never know."

"Oh . . ." I scoff, popping a brow. "Believe me, I know. But sure, let's add it to the pile. What's one more?"

"That's my girl." She eagerly hangs the dress beside the others I have chosen, or more like they *have chosen. There are a good ten*

dresses waiting for me and I only picked two. I'll be honest, I'm not much of a try-on-hundreds-of-outfits kind of girl. But it's for my wedding, so I want to be sure I get the right one.

"Oh my God," Aida gushes, running her hand past a sweetheart lace dress. "Look at this one."

"Okay. Fiiine." I huff out with a small laugh. "I'll try that one on too."

Jade strides past us, holding an ivory gown with sparkly straps falling off the shoulders.

"Not you too!" I slap a hand over my face.

"Sorry?" She grimaces as she tiptoes to hang the dress next to the rest.

"Okay, group meeting," I tell them, raising my palms in the air. "I officially have thirteen dresses there and I'm calling a stop. So get your butts on that sofa, ladies, because I'm heading straight to the dressing room."

"All right." Chiara runs her fingers past another white gown. "But you may wanna see this one. It's got a rhinestone belt."

"Nope." I lift a finger in the air. "No. Not doing it." I rush to grab a few dresses I've gathered, and Brianne, the saleswoman, hurries over to me from around the counter and assists me with the rest.

"You should at least try it on," Chiara calls even as I dash to the back of the store, toward the dressing rooms.

"Not happening!" I burst out over my shoulder, my voice traveling to them.

As we enter the suite, Brianne hangs all the dresses in the large space. "I'll be right outside to help you, just let me know when you're ready."

"Thank you," I tell her as she exits, closing the door behind her.

I take my time, looking at all the dresses, lining them up from most to least favorite, and the one Chiara picked out, well, that's going all the way to the back.

The one I decide to try on first is the one that made my heart skip a beat as soon as I saw it. Strapless and fitted with a dropped waist, the intricately woven floral lace reaches all the way down the swooping train.

Removing my clothes, I place them over the loveseat in the corner, and as soon as I take off that dress from the hanger, I grin.

I step into it as soon as I place it on the floor, dragging it up and holding it against my chest, my smile widening.

"Brianne," I call.

The door instantly opens. "Oh my," she gushes, her gaze taking me in. "That looks like it's been made for you."

She helps secure the corset back, tightening it to give me an hourglass shape.

"I really think this is the one."

"Me too," she says from behind me.

"Could you tell me how much it is?"

"Oh . . ." She waves a dismissive hand. "Mr. Cavaleri informed me not to tell you."

"It's okay." I turn to her. "I won't tell him you told me."

"I don't know. He was very specific." Her fingers go to her side bun, all the blonde hair perfectly coiled, not a single hair out of place.

"It'll be between us." I don a smile, hoping she tells me.

"Okay. But you didn't hear it from me."

"Got it." I tighten my lips for effect.

"It's twelve."

"Twelve hundred?" That's definitely reasonable.

"No," she laughs. "Twelve thousand."

"Oh my God." My brows fly up. "There's no way I can get this."

"It's up to you." Her lips thin into a smile, a thick eyebrow bowing. "But it'd be a shame for him not to see you in it, especially when he insisted that I not let you out of this store until you're happy. And from the looks of it, this dress? Makes you very happy."

I huff out defeatedly, staring at myself once again. It is pretty and he can easily afford it . . . but still.

"How about we go show your friends and see what they think?"

"Okay." I follow her out, my heart racing, strutting in my three-inch heels, feeling like a million bucks.

Chiara's mouth drops as soon as she sees me. "Holy. Fucking. Shit."

"Wow," Jade breathes, just as Aida's eyes glaze over.

"You look so beautiful." She sniffles.

Chiara's eyes glaze over. "Forget my dress, this is the one you have to wear."

I stare at myself, my palms running down the floral lace grazing against my fingertips. A matching veil hits my shoulders, my face beaming. I'm internally counting down the seconds until he sees me.

"I can't get enough of how gorgeous you look!" Aida gushes, wiping away a tear. "I promised I wouldn't cry, but I can't help myself."

She leans into my side, her dusty-rose strappy dress looking stunning on her. I wrap her in my arm, pulling her close. "I'm so happy you and Matteo are able to join us."

"We wouldn't miss it for the world."

"Mom!" Robby calls, running into the room, looking for Jade.

"Daddy said to get the rings from you now." Chiara finishes fluffing my dress as we turn to him, excitement riddling his face. He takes his ring bearer duties very seriously.

"Oh, no!" Jade's face twists with a scowl as she peers up at me with a coy smile, then turns her attention to her son. "I don't know where in the world I put those things." She looks behind her, under the fluffy pillow in my bedroom.

Robby laughs, not buying it at all, glancing up at Aida who zips up her lips. "Come on, Mom! I know you have them!" He grabs her black handbag and opens it as she laughs, attempting to take it back but fails.

"Ha!" He yanks out two ring boxes. "I knew it!"

Her eyes enlarge, her features melting with joy. "Completely forgot that was there."

"Ha. Ha." He narrows his gaze.

"Get over here, you." She tugs him to her, kissing the top of his head. "You look very dashing in your tux."

He fixes his bowtie, tipping up his chin. "Dad said I look even better than he does." Pulling away, he stands up tall. "And considering how good he looks, that's saying a lot." He even imitates Enzo's voice, which cracks us all up.

Jade rolls her eyes with a smile tugging. "That does sound like him now, doesn't it?"

"Damn, if that's not Enzo, I don't know what is," Chiara throws in with a snicker. He's growing on her more and more though, even while she doesn't quite want to admit it.

With a small knock, Janet enters the room, donning a long black gown, her strawberry-blonde hair pinned up in a tight bun. "It's time, ladies." She smiles and my pulse ticks up, my breath leaving in a whoosh.

Jade gets to her feet, holding Robby's hand as she sets to go.

"Thank you again for playing the piano for us. I feel so bad you're not an actual bridesmaid," I say.

She tilts her head to the side. "I love to play, and playing for you all, it's a gift." Her eyes water. "For someone who never thought she'd play again . . ." She places her free hand on her chest, her long French nails biting into her chest. "I'll see you girls out there." Together with Janet and Robby, she walks out the door.

"I can't believe I'm wearing pink," Chiara sneers. "What has become of me?"

"You've become domesticated," Aida jokes.

Chiara scoffs. "Not in this lifetime."

Our soft giggles swell into the emptiness of the room until we set to go, making it down the corridor, the sound of a soft melody echoing closer. I could listen to Jade play all day long.

As we near the glass doors, leading out into the yard, I find Robby waiting there, along with the guys.

"You look great," Enzo tells me, getting Dom and Matteo to nod in agreement.

"Thanks, guys." My chest rolls with a deep breath just as one of the guards we still employ opens the doors.

A grinning Matteo hooks an arm through Aida's, whispering something in her ear before marching down the aisle. Then it's Chiara's turn, both Dom and Enzo walking out with her.

I kneel before Robby. "You ready?" I ask, placing a hand on his shoulder.

He slaps a huge smile onto his face. "I promise to bring the rings down safely."

"I have no doubt." I wink, getting to my feet, and with another excited look my way, he proceeds, as all eyes are on him—all thirty of them.

My boss, Kerry, and a few friends from work are here, along

with some of Dante's employees and business associates. After I texted Kerry, letting her know I won't be able to return to my residency position, I called her again after my uncles were dead, and I begged her to meet me. I wanted to explain everything, to get another chance. She was hesitant at first, but then she invited me to her office.

Of course, I didn't tell her the entire truth, just bits I could share. At first, she refused to give me another chance, but I kept trying. I called. I emailed. I showed up, again and again. She's always been tough, but compassionate, and I was hoping to find that side of her. Once I did, she gave me my position back, but I had to start all over again, which was fine by me. All I ever wanted was to become a doctor, to live a life I had chosen for myself. Now I have it all.

The music changes as Jade plays "Come Away with Me" by Norah Jones, and it's finally my turn. I can't wait to see him, to touch him. My stomach is literally flipping.

Tightening both hands around the bouquet of lilies, I start through the doorway with a single step, until the warmth of the sun hits my face.

Everyone rises, but they quickly melt away as soon as I see him, a hand falling around his mouth, emotions etched within his eyes as they fasten to mine.

With a shaky breath, I continue toward him until I'm near enough to find his love for me shining brighter in his gaze.

"Wow," he whispers, cutting the rest of the space between us. He grabs my face within his strong hands, his eyes gleaming, and it's not from the rays of sunlight bathing the sky. It's from his love for me.

He leans his mouth to my ear, his breath tickling up my neck. "You're the most beautiful woman I have ever seen in my entire life." His lips land softly under that spot beneath my earlobe. "I'm never gonna forget this moment for as long as I live."

He backs away, unable to stop staring at me, and all I manage to do is stare back. "You're my warmth on a cold day, and the strength when I'm at my weakest," I say. "Without you, I'd never know what happiness is. I love you, Dante," I pant, my own emotions swirling in my heart. "Your kindness is the most beautiful thing of all." I circle a hand around the back of his neck, staring deep into his eyes before we realize, the place is pin-drop quiet.

With a fluster, I look around and everyone's smiling at us. My cheeks flush and he squeezes my hand tighter. "It's almost like no one else exists but you," he tells me.

My stomach turns, my heart going along for the ride. Because it's true. He's my entire world.

"Looks like you two already said your vows." Enzo quirks a brow as my eyes quickly flick to my left.

But Dante doesn't even look at anyone else, his mouth winding up, his intense gaze holding mine. "I've said my vows from the moment I met her."

I suck in a breath, my eyes watering over as everyone else gushes. This man and the way he loves me—it's magical. It's beautiful.

There is so much love around us, it's palpable, an energy taking its own life. Love between husbands and wives, between lovers, a mother and child—for once, we're all where we're supposed to be.

How we feel in this moment is how I wish we'd feel for the rest of our lives, though I know that's not realistic. Life sometimes does have a wicked sense of humor, but even still, I want us to remember how we feel right now and take it with us through the trials fate may throw our way.

When the officiant starts, our attention finally falls to her, and with our hands clasped, we marry one another once again, knowing our life is only just beginning.

Three

RAQUEL
FIVE YEARS LATER

"Sweetheart, you're about to pop that baby out any day now," Dante says from beside me, grabbing a bag of grapes and throwing it into our shopping cart. "You should be home resting, with your feet up, not out food shopping with us."

My lips thin into a tight smile and I arch a single brow at my sexy husband, who right now, is doing a great job at irritating a very uncomfortable me. "I need this son of yours to come out like right now, and the doc said to walk. A lot. So that's what I'm trying to do."

"What do those docs know anyway?" He wraps the small of my

back with his strong arm and kisses me softly on my lips. "That kid is a Cavaleri, baby. He's gonna come out when he feels like it."

I scoff, pushing him away playfully, but he chuckles, tugging me to him once more. "Well, you better have a talk with our boy because he's now two days past due and his mama is growing achy and crabby."

"But still beautiful." Dante leans that mouth close to my ear, our eyes on Carnelia as she grabs some raspberries and throws them into the cart. "Promise when we get home, I'm gonna run you a nice warm bath, and when she goes to bed, I'm gonna rub the shit out of your feet all damn night."

A smile radiates my face as I let out a feathery sigh or maybe it was a moan that escaped me. "Did I mention, I'm obsessed with you?" I tell him, my head falling over his shoulder.

His laughter is warm and husky as he kisses the top of my head. "I love you too, sweetheart." This man—he makes me so happy. So content.

In these past few years, he's been the most amazing husband, especially recently as I navigated this rough pregnancy. Between the constant back issues and my blood pressure being higher than they liked, the doctors have kept a close eye on me this time around. And in the past couple of weeks, I haven't been in any mood to have sex. This is the first time it happened in all the years we've been together. I was honestly nervous it'd ruin our marriage, but he's been more than understanding. All he wants to do is take care of me. He cooks for me and gives the most amazing massages.

God, I miss him.

I hope my sex drive comes back after the baby. We never struggled this way with Carnelia. We made the time, even while her sleeping was far and few in between.

"You're a great mom, baby." He tugs me tighter. "That boy is going to love you as much as we do."

"You're a great dad too," I whisper, swelling with an ache behind my eyes. "And the most attentive husband." I lift my head, turning to him, my hand holding his cheek. "In all our time together, I've never regretted a moment with you. You're everything I could want in a man, Dante. I'm lucky to have you."

He clasps a rough palm to my nape, his gaze searing into mine with so much affection, I drown in it, forgetting where we are, even for those single moments.

Dante kisses me softly, and I melt into our love.

"Mommy?" Carnelia's voice drifts from beside us.

Dante groans, reluctantly pulling away.

"Yes, bab—?" I look toward her direction and my heart sinks. "Where is she?" I frantically ask Dante, snapping my gaze all around us. My pulse races a mile a minute, my hands growing ice cold.

"Carnelia? Where are you, baby?" I shout, my feet already moving. As people start to look our way. Dante is marching right next to me. "She was just here," I anxiously say, swallowing the dread scraping up my insides.

"She probably went to the candy aisle." He laughs, but I can tell he's nervous too.

My heart pounds, my body hot and cold all at once. "Carnelia? Where did you go, baby?" We wander haphazardly down the produce aisle, heading for the candy section.

"Baby, it's okay," Dante tries to reassure. "She has to be here." But that does nothing to help me because my daughter isn't here.

I'm trembling, running down the nearby aisle, looking both ways, not finding her anywhere.

"Carnelia!" Dante yells. "Come on, baby girl. This isn't funny."

I choke on my fear, ready to tell him to inform the security and police.

"Mommy, I'm here!" she shouts and my breath catches, my gasping breaths slamming into my chest while I'm running toward her voice, tears swarming in my eyes, my throat throbbing from the heaviness of my emotions.

I don't care how damn huge I am, I run like I've never run before. When I see her, all the blood from my face rushes out.

"Carnelia." The word is a sharp bite as I glare at the person standing tall next to our daughter. "Go to your father. Right now."

"But, Mommy, I was getting my ball from—"

"Now, Carnelia." I can't even look at her, my eyes unable to rip away from the woman who I once called Mom.

"Carnelia, come here, baby," Dante now says, his footfalls approaching behind me, and she quickly goes running to him.

He places a hand on my shoulder, holding our daughter in his arms. I don't even have to see his eyes to know they carry the same contempt I carry in mine.

I angle in a step, my gaze narrowed. "Stay the hell away from me and my family." Contempt is laced thickly in my tone.

She snickers. "Nice to see you too, dear." Her long fingernails run through her blonde highlights. "Not sure what you're going on about. I was minding my business when she ran right into me, chasing this ball here." She stares at her hand, containing my daughter's pink fuzzy ball within it. "I was simply retrieving it for her. You *could* say thank you." She glares with scorn, eyeing me with a callous grin she wears proudly. "I see you're having another." She takes a look at my stomach and all I want is to hide my child away from her. Both of them.

"What happens to me is none of your concern," I stress, trying like mad to control my heavy breathing, but it's impossible. I haven't seen or spoken to her at all since the last time we talked on the phone while I lay in the hospital thanks to her after what Carlito did to me. "I'm glad I didn't take any of my motherly lessons from you."

"Not sure how much of a good thing that is." She arches a mocking brow.

"Who is that, Mommy?" Carnelia asks, loud enough for that evil woman to hear.

"I'm your gra—"

"Don't you ever say that word to her." My voice rises, people scattering past us, sensing the tension. "You'll never be that to my children. Do you understand me?" I take another step forward. My heartbeats pounding through me, making anger and nausea swirl in my gut. "You mean nothing to us. You never will." Dante's hand suddenly tucks in mine, and he gives me a reassuring squeeze. "If I see you next to any of my children again, you better turn the other way and pretend you don't know us. Daddy wasn't the only one with connections. We have friends everywhere, and with a flick of a finger, I can have an order of protection drawn up against you. Or better yet, have you thrown in prison for just about anything I can dream up." Anger roils in my chest, my bitter smile tasting like victory.

She laughs cruelly. "Are you that afraid of me, darling daughter?" She flips her hair with the back of her hand. "My goodness, you'd think I'm a criminal. Like your husband." She punctures Dante with a glare, and I swear I'm ready to land a punch into her perfect, white teeth. I'm not the same woman she remembers. She's going to learn that quick if she continues.

Dante's breathing speeds up, but he remains silent, his hand tightening around mine.

"You ever disrespect my husband again," I grit with a snicker, dropping his hand and walking up to her until I'm close enough to whisper the rest in her ear. "I will kill you."

She snorts, laughing dismissively. "You need therapy." The taunting look in her eyes comes quick before her whole demeanor shifts. "Get away from me. Help!" She lifts her hands in the air, her chest flying up and down as she begins to cry, glancing around the store. "Someone help! This woman is crazy!"

"You're pathetic," I tell her, shaking my head. "Always have been. Always will be. I can't wait until you die. Alone," I whisper as she finally quiets, those eyes rounding at me. "With no one by your side. Because that's what you deserve."

That gets her mood to change back to her regular deranged one. "Do you know what I tell people when they ask what happened to you?" she hisses.

When I don't answer, she continues, "I tell them you're dead."

"That makes two of us." A smile wraps around my lips and there's not an ounce of sadness in my heart, because I never had a mother at all.

"Is everything okay here?" a manager asks, his glasses tripping down his nose as he fixes them.

"Yes, Andy, thanks." Dante walks up, clasping his hand with a shake. "My wife and her estranged mother were having a little disagreement." He leans in closer. "The woman is a little . . ." He circles his index finger around his temple.

"Don't you listen to him!" my mother snaps, grabbing Andy's arm, and he gently flicks it off.

"Ahh, do you need help, ma'am?" Andy scratches the top of his balding head.

"She's the one that needs help," she snaps, pointing at me.

"I got this, Andy. We'll get her out of here." Dante gives him that winning smile.

"Ahh, okay. Well, if you need me . . ." He sets to walk away.

"We're fine." Dante grins. "We'll behave. I promise."

"Okay, have a nice day." Then he's gone, leaving us with her.

"Nice try, Mother," I grit.

"We should go, baby," Dante says, coming up to me. "But hear me," he now tells her. "You come anywhere near my family, and the things that I'll do . . . well . . ." He snickers. "Let's just say, you know what I'm capable of already. Except now, I have children to protect from the likes of you."

She pops her chin up, looking this way and that, pursing her lips, fixing her satchel on top of her shoulder.

"And unlike you"—he bends in real close—"I actually know how to protect what's mine."

Her wrath-filled eyes go to us again, but her mouth stays shut. For once, my mother is speechless.

"It must kill you to know I'm happy," I say with a grin. "And that you didn't get anything you wanted."

"Whatever." She dismisses us with a flick of her hand. "I'm done here."

She doesn't even look at Carnelia, and I hate that this happened in front of her. But God, I couldn't hold myself back. I waited so long to tell her off, knowing I probably never would, and when I saw her, it all came out.

She took and she took, to make herself fulfilled in some demented way, while I suffered. My therapist says she's a classic narcissist, and I guess, over the years of speaking to him, I can see it. Now, it's like I'm looking at her with clearer eyes. She's crazy. I don't care what clinical term there is for her, but she is truly insane. She has to be.

She blows out a noisy breath, and with a stare filled with derision, she turns away and marches out of sight, her short heels clacking until we no longer hear them.

"Are you okay, Mommy?"

I face my daughter, throwing a huge smile onto my face, faking it for her. "Of course I am!" I blink back tears. How could my own mother treat me this way? "I have you, your daddy, and soon your baby brother. I'm the happiest mommy alive."

"Good." She nods. "Because whoever that lady was, I don't like her. Not one bit."

Dante chuckles, placing her down on her feet, and she takes both of our hands in hers.

"Me neither, baby," I say as we head back to our shopping cart, still where we left it, and together, we finish shopping and head out the door.

Once we make it back to Dante's SUV, and Carnelia is strapped in her car seat, Dante tugs my hip and pulls me close enough to kiss me. "If that bitch doesn't put you into labor, I don't know what will."

I scoff. "It's the least she can do."

Four

DANTE

"I knew I should've killed her," I say, pacing in the giant-ass hospital room, Raquel on the bed, looking too damn calm for someone about to have a baby.

"Babe, come here," she calls stretching out a hand, the IV sticking out from her arm. "It's going to be fine. You'll see."

I release a heavy sigh, rushing back to her, my hand in hers as I finally settle in the chair beside her bed. I made sure she had the best room this hospital had. She's on a luxury floor, only two labor rooms here. "Which part is okay? The fact that the doc said you have preeclampsia a day after we saw that bitch?"

"I mean, I'd blame her for everything." She squeezes my hand on a shaky laugh. "But the doctor also did say with my BP going up and down during the third trimester, he's not surprised." She brings my palm to her mouth and leaves a soft kiss there.

My heart lurches. Fuck, I'm worried about her.

"Good thing is," she goes on. "This baby is coming and he's fine. I'll be fine too. Don't worry."

"Well, sorry, baby, worrying about you guys is about all I can do right now."

Her eyes grow bright and glossy, her brows drawing tighter as she presses my palm to her chest. "I love you, Dante."

"Me too, baby." A rush of an exhale leaves me in a hurry. I've never been this nervous in my entire life.

When Carnelia came, sure I was a wreck too, but she came fast. One minute, Raquel was having contractions, the next minute, we were in a room and she was pushing. Five minutes later, and that kid was out. I didn't even have a second to breathe with that girl. She's always been on the go. But little man, hell, Raquel is getting induced, and this wait is fucking me up.

"How about you go get a coffee or ahh, maybe tea?" She giggles.

"Babe, stop laughing." But now I'm chuckling too because she's looking at me with hilarity and pity. "I don't even drink tea."

"I think you should start. Might relax you." She giggles, pressing those damn fuckable lips together.

I can't even think about that right now. I know how hard it's been for her this time around, and I keep reminding her how proud I am of her. She's an amazing mother.

The way she's looking at me right now—her cheeks all flushed, bare faced—fuck, I'd knock her up again and again because I love her pregnant. Minus the complications we had this time. But having kids with her, knowing she's growing our children—it does something to me.

"I'm sorry. I clearly suck at this whole 'having babies' thing."

I reach a hand for her, my thumb stroking down her rosy cheek.

"You don't suck at a damn thing, Dante Cavaleri." Her eyes burn with affection, her hand coming to cup mine. "You're allowed to be nervous. This is your baby too."

"It's not just him I worry about." Raw emotions claw at my heart. "If anything happens to you . . ." I swallow against the lodge of pain in my throat.

"Oh, Dante." She slants her head to the side. "I love you. I'm right here."

I'm instantly on the bed beside her, tugging her to my chest, stifling the ache building in my chest. "I can't help it. I want this to be over so I can take you both home." I brush my fingers up and down her arm.

"I want that too. But the doctor said it could be a few hours until the meds start to work. That doesn't mean anything will go wrong."

As soon as we checked her BP this morning and saw that it was high, we went to the hospital and they immediately admitted her.

"I'm supposed to be the one calming you." I peer at her. "Not the other way around."

"Daddies are allowed to stress out too. It's part of the job."

"Daddy, huh?" I wag my brows.

Her gaze turns to a narrowed slit as she pinches her lips and shakes her head. "Yeah, no, don't do that. Literally. No."

I burst with a laugh. "Daddy likes it when you look at him like that."

"Mmm, yeah, no. Still nothing."

"But are you sure?" I wink, teasingly.

"Sooo sure." Her eyes grow large as she shakes her head, her mouth flanking with amusement.

I love making her laugh, and she's damn good at making me

laugh too. It's one of the reasons we get along so well. She's more than my wife and the mother of my kids. She's my friend above everything, and I'd set the world on fire if it messed with her.

There's a sudden knock on the door.

"Come in!" she calls. "Saved by the knock," she whispers at me, biting her lower lip, her eyes still dancing with a smile.

"Daddy can always torture you later," I say just as Jade and Enzo come strolling in.

"Ugh!" she groans before slipping on a grin as they stride up to us.

"Hey, guys!" Jade greets as she leans over to kiss Raquel hello, and Enzo clasps his palm to mine. "We just got here," he explains. "Everyone is already downstairs I see."

"Yeah, they got here a little bit ago," Raquel answers. "You guys know you may be here a while, right?"

"We don't care." Enzo stands behind Jade as she takes a spot on the chair beside the bed. "Wouldn't miss my nephew being born."

"Aww . . ." Raquel teases, slanting her head to the side. "You think if he sees you before your other brothers, he'll like you the most, don't you?"

He jerks his head back. "Shit, am I that obvious?"

The girls laugh, the conversation continuing while my mind is elsewhere. I can't stop thinking about something happening to her or our baby. It's fucking eating me alive.

"Dante?" Enzo calls. "Where the hell did you go?"

I run my free hand past my face. "Sorry." I release a heavy breath, holding Raquel closer.

"How about we go get some coffee and bring the ladies back a cup?"

"Great idea!" Raquel practically jumps to her feet with excitement. "Please take him. And if you got some whiskey stashed somewhere, get him that too."

"Woman, I'm not getting drunk while my son is born." I chuckle.

"Of course." She waves a hand, glancing over at me. "I'm only kidding . . . sort of." She gives Jade a wide-eyed look on that last part, and Jade tries to strangle a laugh.

"I'm on it, sister-in-law." He walks around to me, throwing a palm on my shoulder. "Come on, bro. Wife wants you to chill out."

"Yeah, yeah." I reluctantly rise, not wanting to leave her alone. I cup her face and kiss her forehead. "I love you, baby. Call me if you need me. I won't be gone long."

"I'll be fine. My BP has been great. See?" She points to the monitor beside her.

"Okay." But it's like my mind won't let me believe everything will be okay.

With a long look at her, my brother leading the way out, I leave the room and close the door behind me.

As soon as we're out, I breathe in long and deep, dragging air through my nose.

"Damn, man," Enzo whispers. "You're really bent out of shape."

"Yeah, I can't stop the shit going through my head," I tell him as we enter the elevator, pressing the button for the lobby.

The back of my head meets the wall with a thud. "This preeclampsia has made me scared. I've been reading up on it."

"Bro, if you read anything about anything on the internet, you're going to think you're dying from a fucking paper cut."

I shake my head. "Nah, this is different. I don't get scared of a lot, man, but her BP was so bad when we got here, even the doc went white. They thought they would have to do a C-section, but then it stabilized with whatever they gave her."

The elevator arrives and I follow him out, marching toward the waiting area where Dom and Matteo wait along with their wives.

Enzo stops short before we reach them and faces me. "You gotta believe everything will be all right. If you're too busy stuck in the worst-case scenario, you'll never live in the moment."

I nod, not sure what else to do or say.

"You're having a son, bro. A Cavaleri. He's gonna be alright. Mom and Pop are gonna make sure of that. You know it."

At the mention of my parents, my chest tightens. I still talk to them, all the time. I want to believe they're looking out for all of us. "Maybe Raquel is right. I do need a damn drink."

"Now we're talking." He clasps my shoulder. "I got some in the trunk."

"Of course you do." I chuckle as we start toward everyone.

"I had a feeling you were gonna need it." He nudges my ribs with his elbow.

He's definitely right.

RAQUEL

There was a time when my world seemed impossibly small. When the light faded. When the possibilities only led to my death, the life dwindling, crumbling with every breath.

Until he came.

Until he saved me.

Even when his every intention was to hurt my family, by using me for a marriage he didn't want, he still took care of me.

And while we were both hurting, love found us when it was the last thing either of us thought we'd find.

But in each other, we found something else—a love that created a family. And with every passing year, I find more reason to smile.

With him huddled against me on the hospital bed, we stare into the face of our son, Tristen, our hearts carrying so much devotion and awe, they're ready to split.

Once he left with Enzo, I was ready to bring our boy into the world twenty minutes later. Then, in another ten, he made it out safely. The most beautiful little boy I've ever seen with thick black hair and large brown eyes. He's a perfect blend of the two of us.

"I can't wait for Carnelia to meet him," I whisper as Tristen coos in my arms, sucking on a bottle.

"You know that kid is going to think she's the mother, right?"

"Oh, I know." My soft laughter splits free, and I'm unable to peel my gaze from my son. "She already told me she'll babysit while I sleep."

Dante chuckles. "You in any pain, baby?" He tips my chin up with his hard knuckles, staring deep into my eyes, and the sentiment slams right into my heart. He always worries about me and it's the sweetest thing on earth.

"I'm just fine." I flash him a wide smile. "Thank you, Dante. For all of this. If it wasn't for you, I don't know where I'd be."

"You saved me, too, sweetheart." He brushes a thumb across my lips, glancing down at them for a quick moment. "I have you to thank for the man I am today."

I release a weighty sigh, a smile radiating my face. "I guess we have each other to thank."

"And I will. Every damn day. Because you, Raquel"—he kisses the top of my head—"you're my everything."

"And you're mine."

"Damn right I am." Together, with the new life beating in my arms, we hold each other, cherishing every moment.

RAQUEL
FIFTEEN YEARS LATER - AGE 47

The years have blown by and it's a wonder to sometimes look back on the life we've built and stare at it in amazement.

Dante and his brothers continue to thrive, opening additional hotels and clubs, growing their empires, making their parents and Tomás proud. I wish I could meet that man and thank him for everything he's done for Dante.

As for me, I finally did become a doctor, and currently run my own surgery practice for a good five years now. It took some time to convince myself I could do it though. I think I still held on to that fear, to that doubt, that I was capable of creating something that's mine. I hate to admit it, but my mother's tiny voice was still there, somewhere deep, telling me I was nothing without her. But I am. I always was. She was the one holding me back.

I never saw her again after the day in the grocery store. I bet anything she followed me there. Why else would she go miles from home and shop there. She doesn't live in the same home my father was paying for. A year after my father's death, she was holed up in a small apartment. She could no longer afford the luxuries in life and I bet it was killing her.

And those scars I once carried, in my heart, are nothing but invisible reminders of a past I no longer remember. One that no longer controls me. I've survived it all. I'm here to tell the story. And my family, they're shackled in ruins. The Palermo name holds no meaning anymore, not even among the other families that still exist.

I ball the comforter around my chest, waiting for Dante to come out of the shower. The years have done wonders on him, and my lord, if that man doesn't get hotter.

It's our twentieth wedding anniversary today, and he's planned a surprise for us. I can't wait to know what it is. He's been entirely too secretive about it and it's making me anxious and excited.

He finally exits, his hair still as long and as thick as I first remember, drops of water dripping past the edges and onto his forehead. "You keep looking at me like that, sweetheart, and we'll never leave the house."

"And what if I do this?" I pop a brow, gently pulling the comforter down my body, exposing my breasts.

His jaw flexes as he finds my nipples hard, my breaths rough when I notice his cock jerking beneath the white towel draped around his hard, defined abs.

"You sexy, little thing," he growls, a hand fisting his hard-on beneath the towel.

My breathing grows ragged the more he touches himself, and my hand slips under the blanket and fits around my wet pussy, my clit throbbing for his expert hands to take over.

"Are you touching your pussy under there and denying me the view?" he rasps, jerking himself still. "Show me, baby. I wanna watch." He rips the towel off himself and my lips part when I see his thick and heavy length.

"I need you," I groan, my fingers slipping inside slow, rubbing myself every time I slip out. His exhales are rough as he marches to the bed, ripping the comforter off my body, exposing every bare inch of me for his eyes to feast on.

"That's more like it." His gaze hungrily cruises down from my heavy breasts to where my hands play.

"How does it feel, baby? Is that cunt nice and soaked for my cock?"

"Dante," I cry, arching the small of my back, my eyes aligned with his, loving the way he still looks at me—like I'm the center of his world. And he's always been mine. This man who never let me forget that I matter. That my happiness is important too.

The bed sinks beside me and I find him there, sitting close, watching me touching myself, his gaze growing heavy-lidded, the stubble riding his jaw, vibrating with the gritting of his teeth.

His fingers reach for my knee, pushing it down onto the bed, spreading me open. I fuck myself harder, the throbbing in my core growing. "Yeah, good girl. Just like that. Make yourself come."

I work myself into a frenzy, unable to snap my gaze from his lustful one, the fiery sensation growing over my entire body, tingles spreading down to my toes, the need spiraling.

As I'm about to come, he swipes my hand away, gripping under my ass with his rough palms until I'm lifted to his mouth.

It's all tongue and lips, my fingers clenching the sheets, my heartbeats loud as he enters me with his tongue, flicking it over my clit.

When he does it again, I'm flying, soaring, refusing to land. He lets me soar again, then his body finds mine, and we soar once more. Together.

DANTE

With my hand on her thigh, we drive into the city for the anniversary surprise I have planned for my beautiful wife. I'm surprised Chiara hasn't spilled. That girl is terrible at keeping a secret, but she knew how much it meant to me. I wanted to make this day special.

She shifts uncomfortably in her seat as my fingers sink into her skin, and I chuckle, loving that after all this time, I can still make her squirm.

"Where exactly are we going?" she asks once I find a spot by Central Park, narrowing a playful gaze. "My heels won't survive that grass."

"Then I'll carry you," I say, picking up her hand and bringing it to my lips for a kiss before my knuckles stroke the softness of her cheek. The way she stares deep into my eyes, it sends a chill down my spine. "Twenty years. Can you believe it?" I ask.

"I can." Her affection spills freely from her tone, her brows furrowing. "The way you love . . . it doesn't even feel that long."

"Until my dying day, Raquel. That's how long I'll love you." I grab her by the back of the neck and pull her to me until those lips brush against mine. "And then for eternity after that."

I capture her mouth, my fingers sinking into her hair, gripping tight as she groans for me, her tongue slipping past my lips. Her hands fist my shirt and she moans for me.

My cock aches to get inside, but breathlessly, I pull apart. "Shit, baby. I'd fuck you right here, but we have somewhere to be, and we're already late."

She giggles, peppering my jaw with hunger-filled kisses, before drawing away, desire still perched in her gaze. "Later, then?" She bites into her lower lip.

"Did you even have to ask?" My words hold all the promise of what she has to look forward to.

With a rough exhale, I finally open my door, then come around to open hers, giving her my hand as we exit together. As we stroll across the grass, I'm taken back to the day I proposed.

We were once right here, having a picnic, before I took her to the very same place I'm taking her now.

She lays her head against me as I clutch her in my arm. "Are we heading to the castle?" There's excitement lined in her words.

"I'm sorry we haven't come back here in a while," I say. "I swear I meant to, but the days, they flew by."

"I know the feeling." She lets out a content sigh, circling her arm around my back. "I'm glad we get to go now."

The last time we were here was five years ago when we took the kids with us. Carnelia was twelve at the time and wanted to see where I had officially proposed. She said when she grows up, she wants to get engaged at the very same spot we did. Now at seventeen, she's every bit her mother—smart, beautiful, wanting to become a doctor too. And love, well? It's the last thing on her mind. She kinda hates it right now. Your first breakup will do that to you. Seeing her sad, it has me wanting to do things to a young kid, I never thought I would.

We near the castle and climb up the steps. When we reach the last one, she glances over at me with the widest smile, and together, we climb the rest of the way.

"Happy anniversary!" people shout from all around us, and she almost stumbles against me.

"Dante?" She slaps a hand over her mouth, unshed tears glazing within her eyes. "How did you pull this off?"

Everyone we love is here—family, friends, our children. Now, we'll have another day to look back on, to remember our love, to remind our kids of it when we're too old to do it ourselves.

I cup her face, a smirk melting to my face. "I had some help."

She shakes her head in wonder, taking my hand as we face our guests together.

"He got you good, huh?" Chiara laughs, giving each of us a quick hug, while Dom nods in greeting.

Raquel shakes her head. "You all did. I can't believe you didn't tell me," she tells Chiara, her gaze narrowing playfully.

"Believe me . . ." Her eyes enlarge. "It was hard. It was why I didn't answer any of your calls today."

The DJ begins to play as guests rise from the long, decorated tables, lined with candles and tall vases filled with calla lilies.

Tristen gets up from his table and hugs his mother tight. "You look pretty, Mom," he tells her and she ruffles his hair, kissing his forehead.

"And you look very handsome in your suit."

Just then, Carnelia approaches, wearing the same knee-length flowy dress her mother is, the same one I had bought for each of them for today. Carnelia's face alights with a beaming smile at both of us.

"So . . ." She props a hand on her hip, popping a single brow. "Are you surprised, Mom? Daddy worked really hard on today."

She wraps an arm around my back and I tighten mine against her, kissing the top of her head.

"Beyond surprised. You two were in on it too?"

"Yep." Her chin rises proudly. "I'm the one who chose all the decorations."

"Wow." Raquel's voice tightens with overflowing emotion. "You guys are so good to me."

"We love you, Mom," Tristen says.

"We do, baby," I tell her, my gaze boring into hers, loving this family of mine with every inch of my heart.

"I have one more surprise for you," I say, giving my daughter another kiss before heading toward the DJ booth and grabbing the mic.

"Thank you, everyone, for being here on this special day for Raquel and me. See, today isn't just our anniversary, it's a day where we get to do it all over again." I slip my eyes to the woman I love, her gaze widening. "I always told you that I would marry you all over again, but today, I get to keep that promise, baby, and this time, it's with our amazing children with us. So, what do you say, Mrs. Cavaleri?" With the mic in hand, I tread up to her, getting down on one knee. "Will you do me the honor of marrying me one more time?"

She gasps on a cry, her fingers trembling as they find her mouth, tears sprinkling into her eyes when I remove a box from my pocket and reveal the ring I gave her years ago. Except, there's a new diamond there, something a little bigger to symbolize our growing love.

I had told her I was going to have it cleaned a week ago, but little did she know, it was all part of my plan.

"What do you say, baby? Would you marry me again?"

She nods frantically, her features softening. "I'd marry you every single time you ask." Her voice cracks, more tears drowning in her eyes. "Every single time."

"That's a good thing." I chuckle. "Or the next part might have been awkward." Everyone explodes in laughter, cheers, and whistles. The sound of clapping envelops around us as I slip the ring on her finger. As soon as I rise, I circle my arms around her, pulling her flush against me, and slam her mouth to mine.

More celebration explodes and I almost forget why we're here until it starts to quiet and the wedding officiant clears her throat behind me—the same one we used on our wedding day.

"Dante . . . this is . . ." Raquel cries, swiping under her eyes. "I'm speechless."

"Are we ready?" the officiant asks. "Or do we need more time?" There's a glint of a knowing smile on her face and Raquel's cheeks grow pink.

I tuck her chin in my palm and turn her face to mine. "I've always been ready."

"Okay, eww," Carnelia says from my right. "Could you guys not make out again until, like, after we're all gone?" Her tone slinks with revulsion.

More laughter breaks and we're both laughing too. And because I'm that kind of dad, I snap a hand to the back of my wife's neck and kiss her like mad.

Part III

ENZO & JADE

One

JADE
ONE YEAR LATER

Once upon a time, the walls caged me in, but now, they hold all the things that matter. It's been a year since Agnelo died. And if Enzo hadn't assured me he was truly gone, I may not have believed it.

I've spent years terrorized by him, living under his shadow, fearing for Robby and me. But we're both safe now, together. With Enzo as my husband, I've never felt safer.

We've been married for four months now and there are still days I have to remind myself that this is really my life. That I didn't somehow dream it up. But his loving arms and the soothing ways he speaks to me when we're alone in bed together, they remind me that I've finally found my home.

I slip into a pair of stilettos, readying to go to work while he sits on the edge of the bed, shirtless, and gazing up and down my body like he's undressing me already. Through the mirror, I find the wickedness lurking beneath my husband's fierce gaze. "Don't you dare look at me that way." I fidget with the sleeves of my blouse, a shiver racing down my back. "I have to go to work," I toss out, avoiding him now as I wind around to the closet, shifting through, looking for a handbag.

He rises off the bed, and my nipples instantly harden beneath my bra, those footfalls heavy. That firm chest presses into my back. I see him behind me through the mirror, and without leaving my gaze, he wraps a hand around my throat, putting pressure, enough to fuel my nerve endings, making me tingle and ache.

His other palm curls around my hip, his mouth dipping to the slope of my ear. "You've got no idea what you do to me." His gaze is a darkened lull of obsession as they take me in through the mirror. I drown in their melody, my flesh his for the taking.

"Enzo," I groan, my ass rubbing over his hardened length, thick and heavy under his gray sweats.

"You keep saying my name that way and I'm gonna drag you to the floor and fuck your pretty mouth until it's dripping with my cum."

"Oh lord . . ." I gasp a moaning breath, dropping my head back against his chest. His dirty talk always sets me off. "It's not fair that you're doing this now, when I have to be at work." I sigh.

"Good," he hums as those lips sink to my neck, teeth biting, lips kissing me there while I cry out for more. My hand snaps to the top of his head as he says, "I want you to think about my fat cock fucking you all day." He kisses me again, sucking on my skin, as those eyes burn into mine. Watching him, watching me . . .

my God, I want this man now. "I want your pussy aching for me when you get home. And when you're back with me, I'm gonna spread you open and feast on your pussy like it's the last goddamn meal I'll ever get."

"Ugh!" I grumble in frustration.

A masculine hand glides from my hip and down my thigh, fingers fledging up my inner thigh until those fingertips brush across my pussy. Even through my jeans, I can feel the weight of his touch.

"Enzo . . . please," I beg, forgetting my job, forgetting everything but him. He sucks on my earlobe. The vibration of his growling makes my core throb.

"I'm gonna be hard all day thinking about your wet cunt riding me. You know how much I love to watch you when you fuck me."

"I soooo hate you right now." My voice is barely recognizable.

His masculine chuckle only makes me ache more. "I bet you do." He backs off, slapping my ass hard.

I spin around, planting a hand on my hip. "You're trying to torture me, aren't you?"

He winks with a smug smirk, and when my eyes lower to the bulge in his sweats, it jerks.

Growling, he pushes up on me, grabbing my jaw. "You gonna keep staring at it or are you gonna get on your knees and finish me off?" His voice is heavy with guttural desire and the sound of it only makes me hungry for him.

I round a hand to his ass and squeeze. "I guess I'm not the only one who's going to have to wait for it." There's a challenge in those words as I let a playful laugh slip. I kiss the tip of his nose and fix the collar of my shirt.

He drops his hand, his chest rocking with heavy breaths. When he gazes at me with scorching intensity, I almost melt for him, almost beg him to do what he's promised to do when I arrive home.

I glance at the clock above his head, and ball a fist in frustration, knowing we definitely have time for nothing. I have to get to work, and considering it's my place, I kind of need to open it.

"I really hate you right now." I practically pout.

He takes my hand and kisses my knuckles. "I love you more, baby." He winks. Just then there's a knock on the door, and he shifts around to hide his erection.

"Come in," I say, exiting the closet, Enzo hiding behind me.

Robby strolls in, holding his tablet. "Morning, Mom, Dad."

Dad.

That one word, it melts my heart, and I know it makes Enzo so happy. But that's what Enzo became, my baby boy's father. Three months after I got Robby back, Enzo asked us if he could adopt him. Robby was beyond thrilled. He was already obsessed with Enzo, and to have that man want him, choose him . . . my God, it meant everything, to the both of us.

My eyes fill with tears as I recall when it became official. Enzo even threw a party to commemorate the event.

"Morning, bud," Enzo says.

"Morning, baby," I say. "Are you two still going to the baseball game later?"

Robby looks at Enzo, kinda suspiciously, and I throw a curious gaze behind me, then back to my son.

"What?" Enzo asks, flipping his hands in the air with a grin.

"Ahh, what was that look Robby gave you?"

"I have no idea what she's talking about." Enzo widens a stare at Robby, tightening his mouth to stifle the smile.

"Yeah, Mom. No idea what you're talking about."

"Uh-huh." I squint at them both, and Enzo playfully nods at Robby with a wink. "Well, I have to go now, boys. Don't eat too much junk at the game."

"We promise not to stuff our faces with lots of ice cream and cotton candy." Enzo winks at Robby who only laughs.

My laughter is low as I stare at the two boys I love more than anything. With a deep sigh, I say, "You two have fun." I lean over, kissing Robby, then leave one on Enzo's cheek.

"I'll miss you," he whispers as he grabs my jaw and captures my lips in a hard kiss, strangling on a groan set deep in his throat.

"Eww!" Robby gripes, and we both chuckle.

"Sorry," Enzo says. "But I kinda love your mother."

Robby grins as we start to walk out, and suddenly his arms swing around Enzo's middle in a tight hug. "I'm happy you're my dad," he says, his features sincere, and my heart lurches.

"Shit, man," Enzo chokes up, clearly not expecting that. "You trying to ruin my cred and make me cry?"

I swipe under my eye. Robby had gone through so much thanks to those monsters, his relief at feeling the safety in the arms of his parents makes sense. His counselor had said he has made great progress, and his school psychologist says he's adjusting great in school. He already has made so many friends. How could they not love him?

Having Aida close by definitely helped Robby in the beginning. She was the only constant he had growing up. I was thrilled when she and Matteo bought a house on the block. Luckily it had gone on sale not too long after, so they were able to move out of Chiara and Dom's place. I'm glad Aida and Robby have remained close. She's like his big sister, and the love he has for her is something that needs to be nurtured. After all, she saved my son in a way no one would've. She loved that boy like her own and I will never be able to repay her for that.

"Okay, you two. I really have to go now."

"Love you, Mom." He waves at me.

"Bye, baby girl. Think about me." He sucks the corner of his lip into his mouth, and holy hell, I ache with renewed fervor.

"You . . ." I tighten my mouth, grabbing his face and kissing him again, giving another one to Robby on the top of his head.

"Behave, boys."

"We will!" Robby calls as I step away.

"We won't," Enzo throws in just as I make it out the door.

Most survivors of trafficking are not as lucky as I am. If they do survive, they don't have anyone to help them transition from that life into the real world.

My idea came to me three months into living with Enzo. I envisioned a place that could offer survivors everything—from a place to live, to counseling, to programs that teach them life and work skills they could take with them to become integrated into the society they were ripped away from.

At first, I didn't think I could achieve what I wanted. It felt too big. But after spilling my heart to Enzo one night, he assured me he had my back and supported me one hundred percent.

He convinced me I had to do it. That a place like that would be a great help to other women, especially when run by a woman who understood what it's like. I wanted to focus on women because many of them wouldn't feel comfortable sharing sleeping quarters with a man, even if he was on a different floor. I wanted to provide safety, not fear.

So, with Enzo's help, we found a place within a week—a three-story building with offices on the first floor, perfect for lectures and workshops, and the upstairs serving as living space.

We quickly found another location, with the intention to

provide both places with housing and programs. Six months after that, Helping Hand was born—a nonprofit organization that has grown more in these first few months than I ever envisioned. With the connections the Cavaleris have, with the funding their wealthy colleagues and friends have provided, it's become a thriving refuge for many survivors.

Seated at my desk, I scan the inventory on my laptop, then proceed to order more cases of shampoo and conditioner, among other things the women here desperately need. The amount of donors we have is miles long. It makes the women feel good, knowing there are people out there who care about them.

There's a small knock at my door.

"Come in," I say and the door slowly parts. I find seventeen-year-old Elena there.

"Ms. Jade, I—ahh—n-never mind." She steps back out just as quickly as she came in.

"Elena, please, come in." I rise to my feet, going to her, towering over her small frame. "You're not bothering me. Whatever it is, I'm here to listen."

She timidly glances up at me, flicking her light brown hair away from her face, the round black and blue around her blue eye no longer there. She came to us three months ago. At first, she wouldn't stay.

She left twice before she came back again, beaten and bruised, after returning to her pimp. The same man who sold her for thirty dollars a pop, allowing men to do whatever they wanted for thirty excruciating minutes. There are marks on her that will never vanish. Her thighs, her back, branded with scars. But the scars on her soul, those are the ones she holds tightly to.

She barely ever talks at group therapy. It's hard. Not everyone can speak about what they've been through.

Elena has no one. Her father abandoned her family when she was too little to remember him, while her mom preferred the company of drugs and men to her and her older brother. Jason, her brother, has been in prison for years. She has nothing to return to. So it's no surprise she'd return to a man like that.

Her abuser has been arrested, and she's supposed to testify against him, but I worry about her, having to relive her emotional trauma.

"Let's go sit," I tell her, leading the way to my bright yellow sofa. The girls here tease me about it, but I love it. Aida picked it out. She said it reminded her of the sun. We all need a little sunshine in this place. "Want some water or iced tea?" I ask, turning toward Elena as she settles on the furthest corner.

She shakes her head, glancing at her lap, picking at her nails. "I'm okay." She doesn't say anything for long minutes and I let her be. She'll find her voice when she's ready, and I'm here to listen. I may not be an official counselor like the two I employ, but I talk to the women every chance I get—in group, in the lectures we host. I haven't shied away from my story. I gave them every raw detail, so they know that they're not alone in this, and that if I can make it through it all, they can too. It physically hurts when some of them leave. I want to find them to tell them to come back. That they're worth more, but nothing I say will make a difference. They have to want this for themselves.

The abusers are gifted at dismantling the self-esteem of their victims. They know how to push at their inner turmoil and peel at the skin that already aches with their demons.

Many of them come from a life that's been riddled with horridness, and once they find someone who promises them a better life, they cling to that.

Others were kidnapped like I was, taken in broad daylight or in the stark of night. Some were found by law enforcement, others were arrested and came to us from prison, or referred to us from organizations that didn't have all the resources we do. In any case, I'm glad they're here, all fifty of them.

"Does it . . ." She finally speaks, the words catching in her throat before she tries again. "Does it ever go away?"

"Does what go away?" I crouch my face down, hoping she makes eye contact.

"The hurting." She looks up, her eyes drenched with tears. "Does it every stop hurting? Because it still hurts, Jade." Her lower lip quivers.

My own tears come, unhurried waves of grief. Taking her hand in mine, I tighten my grasp. "It eases," I say, softly and honestly. "Like a cut that heals with time. You may still see the scar, feel it against your fingertips, but it doesn't hurt as badly anymore when you remember how you got it." My mouth tightens into a mournful smile, my brows knitting. "That's how it's been for me. I used to cry all the time. I cry less now." She glances at our joined hands before meeting my eyes again. "That anger, the rage you feel," I continue. "It's normal, Elena. It's cathartic even. Don't hide from it. Embrace it. But don't let it consume you. Because that'll only let them win." I take her other hand in mine. "And we can *never* let them win."

She nods as she lets out a whimper. "Th-th-there's no one," she cries, tears leaking from the edges of her eyes as she pierces me with the shattering of her pain. "Not one person out there who gives a shit about me."

"*I* give a shit about you," I tell her with conviction in my tone. "A lot of shits actually." The room fills with my small laugh, and she gives me one of her own. "I care very much about you, Elena. I always will. And I know Sasha cares about you too," I add, speaking of her roommate. "She's told me so plenty of times. She said you're a great friend, and that she doesn't know what she'd do if she hadn't met you here."

That gets a smile going on her face. "She really said that or are you busting my chops?"

"You wanna go ask her?" My smile pulls at my features.

"Nah." She shakes her head. "I believe you."

"I'd never lie to you. We don't do that here."

She pauses with a stark look in her eyes, her mouth fluttering like she's nervous to ask me something.

"What is it, Elena?"

She purses her lips. "They really took your kid from you?"

"Yeah." I huff out. "They really did."

"Shit, that's so fucked up." She roughly swats the tears from under her eyes. She doesn't show her pain so freely. It's all bundled up inside her, ready to explode. But my hope for Elena is that she learns how to slowly undo the ties that bind her heart. I want to show her that it's okay to let go, for people to see the real her. Because she's beautiful, and I don't speak of her outer beauty, but the beauty she holds within her.

She's learning how to be a cook here, and the chef who teaches the women sees a lot of potential in her. And if she wants this, I'll pay for culinary school. But that's something I can address down the line. She's not quite ready for that conversation yet.

"Those people, they may have taken him away from me for a long time," I go on. "But I got him back. They stole our years, but they haven't stolen all the ones we still have. And you, Elena, you have so many beautiful memories waiting for you. Seize them." Her long lashes flutter as she continues to stare, taking in every word. "And when we talk again ten years from now, I want you to remember this conversation. Because you have the world in the palm of your hand, and I won't ever stop reminding you of that."

She bursts into tears and jumps into my arms, sobbing against me, while I let her. Because tears, they're powerful, freeing, a release of every ugly thing we carry in silence.

Two

ENZO

"How do people eat raw fish?" Robby practically gags even as he tries to keep a straight face. I add some cucumbers and fresh tuna to the rice, ready to roll the sushi, while he does the same with salmon beside me.

I figured cooking together would be a great way for us to spend some one-on-one time. From the start, Robby and I were tight. Even if he hadn't become my son on paper, I'd love him like one anyway. Me being his dad just makes this all the much sweeter. He's a good kid. I couldn't do better if I had chosen him myself.

"Your mom loves this crap. Thank your aunt Raquel. She got her hooked." I chuckle, throwing some avocado on there too.

"I'm never eating this."

"Good. Your mom would never share." I bump him and

he laughs. "Thanks for being okay with sleeping over at Uncle Dante's tonight so your mom and I could have our date."

"I don't mind." He shrugs. "I usually beat him in video games and that means extra ice cream for me."

I laugh. "I see your game. Well played."

"I learn from the best." His mouth flips into a smile.

"I hope you mean me." I narrow a stare.

His brows furrow. "Well, duh."

"Wiseass." I shake my head on a deep chuckle.

My brothers love Robby. He even helps my brother and Raquel with their new baby. Carnelia is nine months old and already beginning to stand. They've got their hands full.

Dom has some too. Twins, only four months old. After seeing how tired he is, I definitely don't want two at once. I can't wait for Jade and I to have some more kids. I know Robby would love a sibling.

We finish making the sushi, then start on the seafood salad. I kinda lied to Jade about the baseball game. Robby and I wanted to surprise her with dinner. She's going to like this, especially when she knows we both made it. Seeing her happy, both of them—it's what I live for.

And that center she runs, helping all those people, I couldn't be prouder. She's a damn hero. My girl. Everything she went through, and to still have it in her to get up and rehash all those painful memories when others talk about their shit, it's beautiful. She's damn special and all mine.

We no longer have an enemy to fight, and I like this side of the world. I don't miss it. But fuck with us and I'll gladly pull out that savage, lying-dormant inside. He's still in there, waiting. But I keep him contained. He's my weapon when I need him.

"She should be home soon," Robby says, washing the cutting

board. "You think she'll be happy?"

"You kidding? She's gonna cry."

"No she's not." He rolls his eyes.

"Oh, she will. Especially when she tastes those brownies we made."

He scoffs.

"Okay, tough guy," I tell him. "How about if I'm right, I get your dessert for the next two nights?"

"That's not fair." He grimaces.

"Fine. One night."

His looks at me contemplative as he considers it for a moment before sticking his hand out to shake mine. "And if I win, I get yours," he challenges.

"Deal." I tip up my chin and shake his hand.

We start on setting up the table—white tablecloth, the gold-trimmed plates she insisted on buying for holidays, laid out on the table, along with some fancy-ass glasses, and a bottle of her favorite wine.

She's purchased lots of things to make my home, ours. And I wanted her to. She should have everything she's ever dreamed of, and I'll always be the man to give it to her.

My damn heart aches whenever she walks into a room, and that feeling, it fills me up more than any of the liquor or the women I used to use to hide behind. I don't hide anymore and neither does she. We embrace everything together.

Once we're done, Robby and I get to the sofa in the den, clicking on the television, waiting for her, knowing she'll be here any minute. She's always on time. Some car show comes on and we get to watching for a few minutes, while my mind drifts to the day I proposed in Bora Bora, three months after we destroyed the Bianchis.

She had told me she wanted to go to the beach. A place where the water is so clear, you can see your feet in it. Her mom never had money for vacations, she explained, so I gave her the first one she ever had and I made it one to remember.

I help Robby get dressed, while Jade is in the bedroom getting ready for dinner on the beach. The air is warm as I button his shirt in the villa I had rented for our two-week trip to Bora Bora.

I want to take them everywhere, have them experience everything they missed out on, especially as mother and son. She never got to hold him as a baby. Never got that time with him she deserved. It broke my damn heart when she told me about the day that bastard snatched him away. Rage filled my veins, and I wished for Agnelo to be alive again just so I could get the pleasure of killing him. But knowing how he died, what Aida did to him, it's a slice of satisfaction, even if it wasn't my hands doing it.

"I wanted to ask you something," I say to Robby. "Man-to-man." He stares up with curious eyes.

I drag in a breath, more nervous than I realized. "I want to marry your mom and I wanted to get your okay."

He instantly grins, like a full-on smile. "Really? You wanna marry Mommy? When? Now?" His gaze darts to the door, Jade behind it.

"Today. Now actually. I kind of have it all planned on the beach already. So, if you say no, it better be right now, 'cause, ugh, it'd be a little weird when they bring the ring out with our dinner. So, what do you say?"

"Yes!" he shouts, then gasps. "Oops," he whispers, staring back at the door "I mean, yes."

I chuckle, my palms landing on his shoulders and I kneel,

looking into the eyes of the boy who I love as much as his mom. "Thank fuuu—fudge."

"Were you gonna curse? I won't tell Mom." He shakes his head, all serious.

"We don't keep secrets from her, okay?"

"Okay." He shrugs as I tilt my head to the side with a smirk.

"Fine," I throw in. "Maybe some secrets should be between us." I wink. "Like the extra cupcakes I give you after dinner when she isn't looking."

"She already knows." He giggles. "She just pretends she doesn't to you."

"Is that so?" I narrow my stare, and he continues to laugh. I love the sound. That's what children should be doing—laughing, having fun. Not be locked up in cages. Fuck. My chest tightens and anger swells in my gut.

I release a deep sigh, still amazed at what I ended up with—a woman I'm insane about and a kid who may as well share my blood. "You know what it means for us once your mom and me are married?"

He shakes his head, and a wide grin rolls over my face.

"It means I can adopt you."

"What does that mean?" He looks curiously at me, widening his stare.

"It means you get to officially be my son and I get to be your dad. Do you think you'd want that?"

"You wanna be my dad?" His eyes swell larger.

"Very much. It would mean a lot to me."

"Could I call you that? Now? My dad?" Tears rain within his eyes, and shit, I feel them too. I swallow hard.

"Yeah, son. You can." I blink rapidly, trying to keep my emotions in check, but when he throws his arms around me, and grips me

tight, I'm lost to them. I squeeze my eyes shut, my breaths rapid.

"I love you, Dad."

Tears roll down my face, and I didn't even know I could do that.

A sniffle comes from behind Robby, and when I look up, I see her, wiping under her eyes. I didn't even notice her come out of the room.

Our gazes meet and her features are overflowing with love. "Hey there, beautiful," I say, just as Robby pulls away and I rise.

"Enzo . . . you're amazing."

"I try. For you, baby." I make it to her, Robby beside me. I tuck her chin in between two fingers, looking deep into her eyes. "I love you."

"I love you. So damn much."

I kiss her, both hands holding her face as I let her feel my love. Reluctantly, I draw back, knowing this will get out of hand quickly if we keep going, and we kinda have a kid staring at us.

"We ready to go?" I clear my throat, my palm running up and down her back.

Her mouth paints with a gleaming smile. "I'm most definitely ready."

"Let's eat."

We make it out of the villa, walking down the bridge to the sand. Robby rushes down before us, while we stroll, holding hands, her long pink dress, flapping behind her.

"What you said back there? About adopting him?" She turns to me, and our walking slows. "Thank you. I was nervous to bring it up. I wasn't sure if you wanted that."

"I want everything with you, Jade. When are you going to see that? I'm in this forever, baby. You two are my whole damn world."

Her eyes water. "You need to stop being so sweet."

"Sorry, baby." I curl an arm around her hips and pull her hard

into my chest, my lips brushing against hers. "I can't do that. Not with you. Not ever."

"Mmm. Can't seduce me right now. Your mouth . . . it does wicked things to me."

"Oh, I know." I run a hand down her stomach, sliding lower until a finger rolls in between her slit. "When he's fast asleep, I'm gonna fuck you on the floor, overlooking the water. And you better not make a sound."

"My God, Enzo."

"Mom! Dad! You coming?" Robby calls.

I quickly drop my touch away, turning to him. "Yes, buddy."

She sucks in a rough inhale, tangling her hand through mine. "He called you dad again. I don't think I'll ever get tired of hearing that."

"Me neither." I smile, meaning it.

Our feet hit the sand and we continue further up to where a table is set with a bottle of wine and food covered with silver covers. A server is there to greet us.

I pull a chair for her just as Robby takes one next to her. "That sunset," she gushes, staring up at the sky, blazing with flames of orange dipped in gold. "This is like a dream. I could never get sick of the view."

"Yeah," I say, staring right at her. "I could never get sick of the view either."

Her eyes hurry to mine, and her brows tighten when she realizes that the only view I ever want to stare at is sitting right beside me. My hand slides to hers and I pull it to my lap, holding it there.

"I'm hungry," Robby whines and we both return our attention to him.

"Let's dig in." I lift the cover off our trays—a bacon cheeseburger and fries for him, while we start on a salad and the

yellowfin tuna with spiced mangos and some kind of purple sauce.

She takes a bite of the fruit, practically moaning. The fork in her hand drifts over to my lips, and I open for her when she slips a piece of mango from her plate into my mouth.

I suck on the fork, eyeing her intensely, and when she pulls it out, her cheeks fill with pink, and those eyes go lustful.

I bend to her ear. "It doesn't taste as good as you do when you're coming all over my tongue."

"Enzo," she groans softly and the vibrations from her voice have me wanting to take her back to our room.

"Eat your food," I command, a muscle flexing in my jaw, wanting to fuck her right on the damn sand.

I try to keep my dick in check as we eat in silence. The resort I had chosen was exclusive, and the part of the beach we're in is just ours. The other villas are distances away.

The server returns once we're done, rolling a tray, carrying three covered plates. "Whenever you're ready for dessert, sir."

"We're ready." I get to my feet, putting our dirty plates on his tray while he places the new ones on our table. With a curt nod, he strolls away.

Suddenly, I'm nervous. What if she says no? What if she's not ready for that kind of commitment? But I have to know. I have to make her my wife, finally. Because she already feels that way. We just have to make it official.

I lift the cover off Robby's plate first, a chocolate mousse cake with a medley of berries, then I go to hers, doing the same. As she takes a bite, I leave my plate covered, knowing the box is there, waiting for me to use it.

Her mouth tips up into a smile as she continues eating the cake, while Robby eyes me with a wide stare when I nervously lift the cover off my plate and slip the black box into my palm. I don't think she saw me do it, but Robby sure did, growing giddy. But once I kneel onto the sand, she drops the fork with a loud clank.

"Wha—" Her eyes grow large, a palm popping over her mouth, Robby grinning as he stares at each of us.

"Baby, I've loved you since the moment we met. I know you know it's true. I felt what we could be then, and I wanted you every moment since. I saw who I was meant to be when I looked into your eyes, and never want to go back to the days before I met you. I want more. I want us to be a family. So . . ." I open the box, a square diamond surrounded by tiny ones glistens beneath the torches around us. "All I need to know now is, will you marry me?"

She jumps to her feet, pushing the chair behind her. Her chest rises and falls as she looks into my eyes, tears dancing around the rims of her eyes. "Of course, I'll marry you, Enzo. You're the half of my beating heart, and I'll love you forever."

With devotion beating through my veins, I remove the ring, keeping our gazes aligned, and slip it on her finger. Taking her hand in mine, I kiss each one of her fingertips while she stares with maddening affection, at me. At a man who never thought he'd ever find the one who was simply waiting for him to find her.

We returned to that same place a month later, but for our wedding this time, with all our favorite people. My brothers were there by my side and Robby, well, he was the best man.

"I think she's here," he whispers, straightening his back as keys jangle right before the door opens a distance away.

Her heels clack as she nears the den, where we wait quietly. As soon as the door shuts and she struts inside, my eyes see her before she sees me. Long waves slope past her tits, her ass round in tight jeans that I can't wait to peel the fuck off her gorgeous body.

She fumbles with her big handbag slung over her shoulder, and it takes her a second to register us in the room. She lets out a startled gasp. "What are you guys doing here? I thought you'd still be at the game."

"Slight change of plans." My lips lift, loving the shock on her face. I can't wait for her to see what I've got in store tonight.

"Come on, Mom!" Robby jumps to his feet. "We got a surprise for you!" He wanders to her with me close behind. She twists her head just then, giving me an inquisitive stare that has me grinning with a wink.

She narrows a playful gaze as Robby practically tugs her to the dining room.

She gasps as she takes in the setup, her brows bending with the softening of her features. "What is this?" she whispers, pulling a breath.

The room is set with dimmed lights, small candles sparkling across the middle of the table, a vase full of fresh peonies at the center.

"We cooked for you!" Robby rushes to reveal what's on the enclosed trays.

"Wow," she gushes, covering her mouth with her fingers. "You boys did this? For me? Together?" Her voice cracks with visible emotion, pressing her palm against her chest. "This is the sweetest thing."

I near her, inspecting her eyes, seeing tears shining, glancing over at Robby who stares at me with a twist of his mouth.

She wipes her eye with the back of her hand.

"Told you she'd cry."

"Oh, man! You lost me dessert, Mom."

She laughs, swiping across her lashes. "What?"

"He told me you'd cry when you saw all this, and I said you wouldn't." He huffs. "This is no fair."

"I'll tell you what, buddy." I fling an arm across his back, pulling him to my side. "I'll let you keep your dessert, but in case we're keeping score, remember who won this one." I nod once, pointing to myself.

"Ha. Ha." He rolls his eyes, humor there.

"You ready to go to your uncle Dante's?" I ask because I need my girl alone for all the things I'm gonna do to her.

"Wait, he isn't staying?" she asks just as Robby runs off to get his overnight bag and shoes.

"Nah." I approach, tugging her jaw in my palm, my lips nearing her ear. "We're playing all night, baby. It's safer if he's gone." I brush my lips right down her neck. "I'm gonna have you screaming my name all throughout this house." I pitch back, our gazes tangled in heated desire, her shallow breaths practically bursting out her parted lips. I steel my jaw, my cock throbbing from the flushed look on her cheeks.

Robby is back. "Ready."

"I'll be back in a minute." Grabbing her nape, I yank her to me, kissing her quickly on a growl of frustration, then we head out the door and I practically run toward Dante's.

"Hey! I can't go that fast," Robby complains as we rush down the empty street in our gated block. I slow the pace on a chuckle. "Sorry, little man. I'm a little hungry."

And it isn't for the food.

"Yeah, well, a kid's gotta walk, so let me walk, old man," he says with a laugh.

"Old man, huh?" I stop mid-step, tilting up my mouth, ready to grab him, but he dashes away. "Not fast enough," I say just as I circle my arms around him and flip him in the air, carrying him that way to Dante's

"Hey!" he yelps with humor. "If I fall and hit my head, Mom's gonna kill you."

"Yeah, yeah, zip it up down there." I carry him that way to Dante's door, knocking with my free hand. My brother opens the door, jerking up his brows.

"Remind me never to ask you to babysit." He shakes his head. "Hey, Robb . . ." He peers down at him. "Want me to kick his ass?"

"Yes, save me!" Robby giggles.

"Drop my nephew. Now." He pretends to get serious, rolling his arms against his chest.

"Fine," I say, dropping Robby to his feet. "But that's only because my lady is waiting for me."

Robby rubs his forehead. "I think all the blood is officially in my skull. Thanks." Dante parts the door, and he runs in.

"All right, you fuckers. Have fun. Daddy's got business to take care of."

"I'd say we'll miss you but . . ." Then Dante shuts the door in my face.

"I know where you live!" I shout through the barrier, then I'm off, rushing back even quicker. When I'm finally opening my door, she's waiting for me, same heels on, but fuck, she's in a completely new outfit. My eyes slowly wander down those curves, wrapped under the fiery red dress she has on, and that heavy bulge in my pants physically jerks.

"Lord have mercy on my cock."

"So you like?" She runs her hands up and down her hips, eyeing me with a seductive glint.

I prance up, running a hand through my hair, blowing a harsh breath, unable to take my eyes off her body. "You sure you wanna eat first?" When I'm in front of her, I curl my palms around her ass, tucking her to my chest, my hard-on pushing into her.

"I am kinda hungry." Her mouth goes all sultry in the way she smiles, a finger twirling a loose strand of her hair.

"Is that so?" I clutch her hips with both palms, lowering my mouth to hers. My lips hover close to the warm breaths slipping out her lips. "What's my girl hungry for?"

"For the sushi you made, of course." Both of her hands climb up my back, her nails biting into the flesh there, causing my muscles to twitch.

I let my lips brush against hers, groaning as she lets go of a small, little moan. "Is that all?"

"What else would I be hungry for?" she breathes.

Growling deep in my throat, I force her body up against the wall with the power of mine. My hand inches around her neck, curling around it, my fingers delving into that soft skin. "For this." I arch my pelvis into hers, my cock rubbing against her, and her hands ball into tight fists against my lower back.

"Enzo," she cries.

"Yeah, baby . . ." I roll my hips harder, deeper. "I know exactly what you need." My lips fall to her neck, kissing and sucking on her skin, grinding my pelvis into her at the same time. "I'm gonna strip you of this dress until you're in nothing but those heels and a pair of panties. Then I'm gonna show you exactly what I'm starving for."

JADE

He loves it when I play, the piano keys against my fingertips, eyes closed as the melody surrounds me like a warm blanket on a cool night.

His hands buckle around my shoulders from behind and his dominant touch seeps through me, my nipples tightening as I let myself get swept into a trance—both from the music and his hands on me. Feeling him, the music, it's all too much, yet not enough. He grasps me harder, massaging me as those hands wander down my arms. I drown in it, all these sensations drifting down my body like a ghostly touch.

After we ate, we somehow ended up in the music room, where he asked me to play. Those warm, soulful eyes, hypnotizing me as he kissed me slow, my back against the piano. When he turned my body around, he forced me down on the bench while I grew achy and needy from the way he demanded with a simple touch that I do what he wanted.

His hands glide down my arms, gradually moving toward my breasts, his thumbs licking past my nipples through the dress— beaded and hard for his mouth. Needing him badly, I push my core into the bench, dying to ease the throbbing in my clit.

"Enzo . . . please," I murmur, my fingers slowing as he pinches my nipples.

"Keep playing." The demand caged in his tone is a beat of lustful pleasure calling to my body, searing into my skin.

I don't stop. I make the music bleed from my very soul even as his hands move down onto my lap. He yanks the dress up as I sit up a little, giving him room. A moan climbs out of me, anticipation drawing me in, desperate for him to touch me.

The silky touch of his fingers brushes against my inner thighs. Finally.

I play faster, wanting this song to end so he can have me.

Crawling, he slides those fingertips higher. My breathing is shallow as he slides up against my core, right between my slit, sliding up and down.

"Oh God," I breathe, losing concentration, my fingers slipping off the keys.

"Don't stop or I stop," he warns. "I wanna hear you play while I play with you."

I swallow the heaviness in my throat, a trail of goose bumps running up both arms, as he slips my panties to the side with his index finger.

My thighs willingly spread, needing the ache to ease, yet knowing it'll return if he wills it so. He owns both my body and my heart. I'm his to play. He's right about that.

"Enzo!" I cry as he grazes my clit with his thumb just a fraction, just enough for me to crave more of it. "Please, I need . . ." My fingers pound on the keys, and I stop playing. Suddenly, he does too.

"No…" I protest. "You can't do this to me."

His deep-chested chuckle, those lips humming across my neck, it sends a jolt down into the space I need him to fill.

"Hands back on the piano. I told you what I want. Now finish."

With a groan, I make my hands work again, playing with fervor, and he finally touches me again. His fingers brush over me, teasing my lips there. I exhale sharply as he eases inside me, just the tip of his fingers and I burn everywhere. "Enzo, yes," I whisper on a moan. A thumb fondles my clit, as he fucks me deeper now, two fingers where one had been.

"Harder!" I cry, the music no longer sounding right, but I don't stop a second as he fucks me, my hips circling, needing more. "Enzo, I'm gonna . . . Oh God!"

My hands tremble against the piano as I cry, my toes curling in the pumps wrapped around my feet. "Fuck me . . . I need you."

"I know what you need," he groans, his other hand fisting my hair, yanking my head back so I can look at the eyes of the man I desperately want.

His teeth grit as he pounds deeper inside me, three fingers stretching me wide until my eyes roll back and I think I stopped playing.

"Yes, yes, yes . . . don't stop. Do-don't . . . ohhh . . . fuck, Enzo!" His name on my lips is a desperate plea for more. Our eyes are fastened as every inch of me scorches up while I fall into the fire he created. I'm quivering against his chest as he looks at me as though he wants to devour me.

I don't stop coming. It's unending. I'm a trembling mess as his fingers wedge so deep, I see stars.

His hard breathing is at my forehead while my body gradually eases, my exhales a tattered mess. He cups a palm around my throat, gripping me in a choke hold as he turns my head back to him, and takes my mouth with his. It's like a damn possession—teeth, lips, growls, and moans. We practically tear each other apart, the passion dripping from the love and sizzling chemistry we have for one another.

His teeth sink around my lower lip, pulling hard enough for the pain and pleasure to feel one and the same. I suck his tongue into my mouth, and he tightens the large span of his palm around my throat in the most delirious way. I crave when he turns animalistic—a man who desires me with ruthless need.

"Stand up," he demands, backing off as I try to get to my feet. He helps me up, his piercing gaze roaming down my body, leaving a path of destruction in its wake. Because I want him again, need him so bad, I'm willing to beg to feel his cock inside me.

Before I can say a word, his hands are on my dress, yanking the side zipper down. "Take it off for me." His eyes grow hooded, my mouth parting as my hands go to my shoulders, our gazes touching the way I want our bodies to. Slowly, I let the dress drift lower, and lower, exposing my breasts to the gaze feasting on me.

His jaw clenches, his chest rattling with heavy breaths. Without taking my eyes away from his, I let the dress glide all the way down, until I'm in nothing but those panties and heels he wanted.

"Fuck, you're goddamn beautiful." His voice slams with an ache as though it hurts to look at me. The emotions on his face—my God, I can feel them.

He comes nearer, a fierce look in his eyes, like a predator waiting to catch his prey. With a rough palm against my stomach, he pushes me back against the piano, then grabs under my thighs and lifts me up on top of it. My ass hits the keys, the music now a haphazard mess, kinda like me.

His hips pull in between my thighs. He cups my breasts with both hands, massaging my sensitive flesh, thumbing over my stiff nipples.

"Please, Enzo . . ." My brows tighten, the walls inside me constricting with heady desire. "I need your cock."

He bends to me, his heavy breathing floundering against my lips as he leans in some more, his mouth against my jaw, his teeth grazing the skin as he pushes his finger into my pussy, inch by tantalizing inch.

I open for him, wanting him to plunder deeper, faster. "Enzo, please give it to me harder."

He chuckles gruffly. "Look at my greedy wife, spreading open her pretty pussy for me as wide as she can." He glides another finger between my wetness, and I arch my back on a moan, the sensation…it's too much.

"Oh . . . fuck," I breathe with a tremble, and he growls deep, grabbing my throat like he owns it. His thumb presses into my pulse, deepening as he plunders those fingers inside me with lazy strokes.

"Fuck me. Please…" My teeth clench, my eyes heavy-lidded. "I've been insane thinking about you on the way home, remembering this morning. Playing it over and over . . ."

He growls, nearing my mouth, kissing me hard, before he lets his mouth pepper down my chest, my stomach . . . He hooks his arms under my thighs, sitting me down on the bench I had just been in and fits his head between my legs.

He meets my gaze, his tongue rolling up from my ass, up to my clit. I buck beneath, the keys singing to a chorus of my cries. His tongue drives deep inside me before his lips lock around my clit, sucking me hard into his mouth.

The desperation of yet another orgasm springs to new life, needing it even more than the last. My clit aches as he licks, nibbles, sucking roughly, his fingers back inside me. I'm not sure how many. I'm too far gone to focus on anything but the desperate desire to get the release I'm chasing. With one more flick of his tongue, I shatter.

"Yes!" My breaths catch in my throat as I scream out, digging my nails into his scalp, pulling his hair as I come. My body shudders as he tastes me, his tongue spearing inside, dragging up to my clit, doing it over and over, working me into a frenzy.

"Mmm," he groans, practically sucking me dry and the vibrations of his voice beat through my body like fireworks.

He climbs up, taking my mouth in a slower kiss this time, and I taste myself as he rolls his tongue with mine.

His palms are under my ass, lifting me off the piano onto legs that don't seem to work.

"Hands on the keys, baby girl," he drawls, and I slowly do as I'm told, bending my ass over for his eager hands. A palm strikes me hard before three fingers pump inside me.

"Yes," I cry breathlessly, needing that man to finally fuck me.

He lets me go, backing up as I eye him from behind my shoulder. He lifts off his t-shirt and tosses it before his hands are on the waistband of his pants. The outline of his thick cock only makes me want to get on my knees and suck him dry. But I want him inside me too much to move.

I find my hand slipping to my pussy, working my clit as I watch him pull his pants and boxers just enough for his crown to peek out.

He drags both down his muscular thighs until he steps out of them. His palm wraps around his length as he groans, watching me touch myself.

But he doesn't let me go far. He pushes his body into me, grabbing a fistful of my hair, yanking my head back. "Who do you belong to?" Our eyes connect as the head of his cock enters me, giving me a taste. "Say it." He thrusts just a little deeper.

"Enzo . . ." I stammer, unable to take how badly I need this.

"Say it, baby. I wanna hear it." His voice seeps with need, for me—his wife. The one he loves. The one he worships. And God, I worship this man. He's my everything.

"I belong to you…just you. My body, my soul, it's always been yours. Only yours. Please, just fuck me." The words fly out in a hurry.

"Good girl," he hums, and that's when he slams all the way inside.

"Fuuuuk!" He slaps my ass with his free hand, while my groans and cries tangle into one sound I barely recognize.

He bucks his hips, slipping out, then in again. My body hits the piano hard, my fingernails pressing onto the keys, creating our own music. Those beastly strokes of his, that hand tightening in my hair, the other spanking me harder, has me climbing, tethering.

"That's it . . . take every inch," he grits, tugging my strands with his fingers, arching my neck for his teeth to wrap around my earlobe. "It's yours."

Then it comes, the plundering waves. They take me until I sink into the bliss, until I'm washed ashore, and his arms wrap around me and they hold me tight. Because with him, I never drown. I never will again.

Four

JADE
SIXTEEN MONTHS LATER

"Slow down!" I tell him as he whizzes past a car on our left. "Unless you expect me to have this baby in this car, Enzo!"

"Shit, I'm sorry, baby." He takes a deep sigh, placing his palm on my thigh and gently squeezing, while I try to control my breathing, another contraction landing in my lower stomach.

I take a swallow of another inhale, trying not to panic, but I can feel it coming, my heart speeding rapidly, my pulse slamming hard in my neck.

Because in this moment, my mind, it goes back to that day. To those awful memories of when I had my son and had him ripped away from me. The aching. The bleeding—my body and my heart—I feel it now, like a festering sore filling me with agony. Carrying another child is hard. Harder than I thought it'd be with my past being as it was. I was a mother without a child, and now, I'll be a mother with a baby . . . will I know what to do? Will I fail her? My daughter. An ache slams to the back of my nose, reminding me of my own mother and her love that still carries me in everything I do.

"We're almost there," Enzo says, his voice now urgent yet soft. He had wanted this baby from the moment I found out I was pregnant. We weren't actively trying. It was kind of like, well, if it happens, then it happens. Then one day, it did.

My beautiful daughter is about to make her entrance and her mom can't even keep it together. But I'm going to try. I want to savor this moment. Growing her, knowing I was loved and cared for. That I was safe. It was something I never had before. But Enzo made sure I knew that every single day. He had me. No one would touch me again.

We finally arrive, and he quickly parks the car, grabbing our bags and helping me out. "Can you walk or should I carry you?"

I laugh even as I grit my teeth from the pain. "I can walk, babe."

He nods, and I reach for his hand, holding it tightly. He glances to me, his brows furrowing, his chest rising and falling. It's cute how nervous he is. It makes me love him even more.

We make it inside, and he demands I be put in a room immediately. He upgraded my room, so I have a suite to myself, and one of the nurses takes me there in a wheelchair, while he proceeds with the paperwork.

Once I'm settled on the bed with the epidural doing its thing, Enzo returns, settling on the chair next to me. A nurse strides inside, wearing pink scrubs, her black hair pulled up into a tight bun, not much older than me. "How are you feeling, mama-to-be? Is the epidural working?"

"Is she allowed to get any more of that?" He quickly rises, rushing a hand past his full head of hair, a few strands draping across his forehead.

I laugh behind him while the nurse eyes me with a twist of her lips.

"I'm fine, I promise," I tell him. My smile is comfortable now, the pain no longer a burden. But he saw me scrunching my nose at a particularly long contraction and he was not having it.

"Well, if you need more, just press that little button on the remote they gave you." She places three cups of Jell-O down.

Enzo practically snatches it and press it once or maybe twenty times, but I think there's a cap they set on that from what they explained. I won't tell that poor man that.

"I'm sorry this is all you could eat, but I got you a few," she tells me. "If you need more, just call for me."

"Thanks," I say while she fills a cup with water, placing it on the chair beside me.

"The doctor will be in to see you shortly."

She walks out and Enzo stops pacing for a moment, staring at me. "You need anything, baby? I can sneak you in some sushi if you want."

I burst with a laugh. "Come sit by me, you big softy."

He runs a hand down his face as he blows a heavy breath. He comes to settle on the bed right by me.

"Are you doing okay? You know, with everything?" he asks, his knuckles tenderly tracing down my cheek. He knows how much I'd had to deal with when they took Robby from me. He knows that being pregnant, the fear that this baby could be taken, had been there, as irrational as that may be. And he's been there for me, loving me through all of this "You're incredible, Jade. I'm in damn awe of you every friggin' day."

A rush of emotions swells in my chest, my eyes brimming with incoming tears. "This is hard," I admit softly. "But I'm okay. You're here this time."

"That's right, I am." He fiercely picks up my hand and kisses my palm, then places it against his chest. "I swear to you on my heart, baby, no one will hurt you. No one will ever take our daughter. She's safe, baby, with us. And so are you."

I sink further into the pounding of the love and aching devotion that seeps through my soul for this man. My husband. The love of my whole heart.

"Hello there." Doctor Andrews walks in with two nurses, and I rapidly wipe under my eyes. His gray mustache flicks up as he smiles. He's comforting to be around, always happy, making jokes. He throws on some gloves, then he's checking how far along I am while I squirm uncomfortably.

"Well . . ." He removes the gloves as he rises to his feet. "You're having your daughter now."

"What? Already?" My eyes grow wide, my pulse throbbing in my throat.

"Well, I think you've waited long enough, don't you?" He chuckles, and he doesn't even realize how right he is. Because I have. I've waited forever to hold my baby, to love her, to keep her.

Enzo lowers his mouth close to my ear. "I'm right here. I love you. You're safe. She's safe."

The tears roll down my cheeks as I nod.

The doctor prepares some utensils on a tray, the lights above me flickering brighter. I pull in a long, deep breath, feeling the force down below, knowing she's going to be here no matter what I want. I do want to meet her. I want to hold her. But I'm scared.

"Okay, when you feel it, push." The doctor is at my feet again, and when the next contraction comes, I do. I push. I scream. I cry. I let myself feel it all—the intensity of this moment, my soul ripping apart inside me, the memories as I screamed for my Robby, lying on that floor with blood still leaking out of me as he was stolen from me.

My body feels it all, the past, the present. It's all a swirl of an avalanche with me in the center.

"I see her head," Doctor Andrews says. "Come on, Jade. Push!"

A scream rips out of me, Enzo's voice reassuring me that I can do it. "You're doing great, baby. She's coming. She's about to meet her mommy."

My vision blurs, and with another groan, I feel as she enters the world. But when she cries, my entire body does too.

"Give her to me!" I shout, my voice crackling like a slow growing fire. "Please." My voice lowers, my chin trembling.

The doctor looks up just then and lifts her in his arms. Once he places her on my chest, I burst into tears, sobbing as she lies there, her hand on my breast, her small body tucked over the safety of mine.

It's the most magical feeling, and that fear I had, the one telling me she's going to be taken away, it melts away into more love than I could ever imagine having for another child.

"Lauralyn Avery Cavaleri." I tuck my palm over her tiny head, naming her after my mother Laura. "Welcome to the world, baby. You're safe here. I promise."

ENZO
THREE MONTHS LATER

There was no way I could ever comprehend what it meant to have a baby, but Lauralyn has taught me a lot in the last three months. Not all of it had to do with late-night bottle feedings or what to do when she won't stop crying. She taught me patience. She taught me gratitude. But most of all, she taught me no matter how much you could love, there's always room for more.

It feels like she's always been here. That the world before her just simply didn't exist. She lies across my chest, Jade sleeping soundlessly beside me, while Robby's in school. Jade has been very overprotective of Lauralyn, and I understand why. I let her do whatever she needs to do to feel safe. Having our daughter now and imagining some fucking bastards taking her, hell, I'd want to burn down the whole damn world. I don't know how she survived. She's stronger than I could ever be.

I kiss the forehead of my tiny angel, her little lips open as she peacefully breathes. Could you stare at someone nonstop? Because I can.

Jade stirs beside me and I hope it's not because she's having a nightmare about the past. She hasn't had one of those since before she got pregnant. Therapy has helped. Her job has too. Helping those women has helped her in return.

I've done all I could to make her feel safe, like finding the third man who hurt her when she worked for those fucking animals. I killed the other two while she watched, but this one—Sammy fucking Rio. I killed him myself a month later.

"Please, I'm sorry! If you let me go, I swear I'll—I'll disappear," he frantically begs, fat tears pouring out his eyes as he sits in the basement of one of our hotels, zip ties around his legs and hands. Two knives stick out of him, one over each thigh.

"Yeah, you will." I snicker, playing with the pliers in my hand, walking up to him, blood seeping out from the large gashes under both of his eyes. "Begging won't help you. Nothing will. Not with me." I dig the pliers under his chin so hard, I draw blood. "You're gonna die painfully, and those kids of yours, that wife who doesn't know who the hell she's fucking, will never see you again."

His sobbing is heavy as I grab his hand, edging the plier to his nail, and he instantly sits straighter. "Wha-what are you g-g-gonna do with— Ahhh!" Gradually, I peel the nail off, taking my sweet time as he continues to scream in terror.

"I'm gonna take everything from you. Because, see . . ." I toss the nail in the trash as Dante holds the man's head steady, so he doesn't continue to rattle the chair. "She's not here, and I get to be as bad as I want to be."

In a flash, I'm on him, punching his cheek, his hand in mine as I peel every single one of his nails. He screams louder, the ragged weight of his gasps growing heavier. I revel in his pain, remembering what he did to her.

"A baton? That's what you did to her." I rip another nail as he shouts in agony. "To my *girl!" I pull off every single one until all ten are gone.*

Raising the pliers to his neck, I shove it into his pulse, and with a jerk, I move them away, then jam it into his neck. Blood squirts out across my face.

"Ahhh! K-k-ki-kill me."

"But I'm having too much fun." I chuckle with a sinister tone.

Dom hands me a razor, a vicious snarl on his face. The razor lands on top of Sammy's ear while I hold it between my fingers.

"No!" He shakes his head. "P-please. You—you can't."

"I can," I grit. "And I will." The slicing is quick, the knife too sharp. Then I'm holding his ear in my hand. I could barely

recognize what he's saying, the sniveling growing louder.

"You can give it but can't fucking take it?" I round a punch to his nose, crimson gushing out.

Dante laughs behind him. "I hope it hurts." His voice is full of virile disdain because when you fuck with one of us, you fuck with us all.

Dom marches over to the black duffel on the floor, removing one of his torches. "You play with fire. You're gonna get burned." He hands it to me.

I flick it on and off right in front of Sammy's face. He could barely look at me, his head hung, the sobs drowning out my laughter.

"I will sleep well knowing you're dead." The torch roars to life one last time, then it's on his face, searing the flesh where his ear had once been. My brutality has no bounds. I burn every inch of his face. I even take his fucking eyeballs and his dick. I should skin him alive for this, but I've done enough.

His screams eventually drown out until his life does too. I hope it brings her some comfort.

Lauralyn rustles above me, her eyes opening as she smiles. "What are you doing up already, princess?" I whisper, her blue eyes so bright, it's like they've been molded from the sky. "You're so pretty." Her gummy smile grows even bigger. "Daddy is gonna keep you safe." My hand rounds her little butt. "I'll kick all those boys' asses. You just say the word. Okay?" Warmth washes over my body.

Her eyelids flutter as they start to close, like she's heard me, like she knows she's protected in my arms.

My family. It's crazy to even imagine I'm here. A wife I'm in love with, two kids I'd kill for.

How the hell do I deserve all of this? What have I done to earn it? But it's mine anyway and good luck to anyone who tries to pry it out of my hands.

It's been three amazing months since Lauralyn was born, and being her mother has filled a void inside me—that emptiness that the Bianchis dug when they took my son away. And though I'll never get back the years they stole with Robby, a part of me has healed when I had her, when no one was there to tear her away from my arms.

I'd do anything to get those same experiences with Robby that I get to have with her. All those firsts I'd missed out on. The first time he smiled. The first time he said mama. The first time he took his steps. The hugs. The kisses. God . . . I can't even think about it all without my heart breaking.

And though I'm grateful Aida was there for all of them, her kindness and love for my boy giving me some relief, still, it hurts to know I wasn't there for any of it.

He missed out on so much of the bonding between us, but I have done everything to make up for it—Mommy and son dates, time alone at home, showering him with as much of my attention as I can.

The thing with Robby is, he's adjusted fine. I'm the one who had the weight of her failures on her shoulders—feeling not good enough, like I failed as a mother. I know none of it was my fault. I know I couldn't change a thing, but I still felt that way.

It took a while for me to let the guilt go. My therapist has been kind of like my fairy godmother. If it wasn't for her, I'm not sure I'd be where I am today.

She has helped Aida too. We both learned a lot about ourselves through her wisdom. We learned how to let go, to embrace the present and tuck away the past. She now works for Helping Hand part-time, helping the women like she's helped us.

I turn the car off, parking it in the space closest to where my mother's grave is. I haven't been here since before I gave birth, and I usually go every month. But it's been one sleepless night after another, and before we know it, it's been three months.

I'd normally go with Robby or sometimes Enzo would come along too. Other times, it'd just be Elliot and me.

Having him back has been like having a piece of myself returned to me. We've gotten really close, and he's over at the house like once a week, hanging with Enzo, Robby, and the rest of the Cavaleris—shooting hoops, barbequing. It's nice that he doesn't live but ten minutes away.

He still works for Dante and the guys, but now it's as security for their growing businesses. They shuffle the men they employ between the nightclubs and hotels they run. That's actually how he met this woman I kinda hope he marries. Dante assigned him to her family while they're here for business for a few weeks.

He's crazy about her, even though he acts like she's just a job. But a sister knows. Becoming an aunt wouldn't be so bad either.

I turn my attention to my children, twisting around to the back of the SUV. "We ready to see Grandma?"

Robby grins, holding a bouquet of pink carnations, her favorite.

I want my mother to meet Lauralyn, someone named after her, someone she would've loved had she still been around. The hurt from losing my mother is hard, especially in the beginning. When I was still in the clutches of the Bianchis, I had pictured seeing her face again, hearing her voice telling me how much she missed me. But I never got that and it hurts like hell. I miss her every day.

She'd be so proud of me and the family we've created. She and Enzo would've gotten along splendidly. She had a sense of humor and he'd make her laugh for hours.

I sometimes imagine it, like it's happening. All of us around the kitchen table—Elliot, Mom, Enzo, the kids. Happy. Fulfilled. Then my eyes open and it all disappears.

Robby unbuckles himself while I get out to get Lauralyn's car seat, and together we stroll down the freshly cut grass, arriving a short distance to my mom's plot. It's a simple headstone and looks like it's been taken care of, pink and yellow flowers already there, probably from Elliot. I know he comes here alone too.

Robby sits right down in front of the headstone, while I place the car seat on the ground, joining him. "Hi, Grandma," he says, and my nose instantly burns, emotions stumbling through my heart— utterly broken yet so full all at the same time. "I have a sister now and her name is Lauralyn. Now we're both named after you," he explains, since he's named after her middle name of Roberta.

Tears slip past the edges of my eyes. She should be here. This isn't fair. She was too young. There's so much she's missing out on.

Her love. Her memory. It's there, within my children. I hope they grow up to be just as beautiful as their grandmother once was. Because beauty, it's what grows inside your soul. And nurturing it, feeding it, giving it life, that's what being human is all about.

ALMOST TEN YEARS LATER

Balloons flutter in the wind, the laughter of children filling the space in between, all of us gathered in the yard of our home for Lauralyn's tenth birthday. She invited the entire class and most of them came, plus all her cousins too. It's a full house, and we have plenty of food to feed an army.

The family is sitting in the large gazebo, Enzo and me sipping on our drinks—Baileys on the rocks for me, a bottle of beer for him. I pass a bowl of pretzels to Chiara, who takes a handful, giving some to Raquel seated beside her.

Kayla and Elsie are here too. Both of them married now, a family of their own. After everything we've been through, each of us has carved a piece of the world and made it ours.

"I swear, if both of those boys make it to their eighteenth birthday, I'll be shocked." Chiara shakes her head, blowing an exhausted breath, her eyes glued to Gianni and Frankie, throwing each other around.

"Are they wrestling again?" Aida asks on a laugh, her head tucked on Matteo's shoulder, his arm firmly around her.

"Sure." Chiara blows an exasperated breath. "If you wanna call it that."

"It's okay," Dom says, throwing an arm around her. "We've got good insurance."

She bites back a laugh.

"So," Matteo says this time. "Are you all joining us on Corvo Island this summer?"

"Hell yeah," Enzo answers. "Can't wait."

"Hey, Mom. Dad." I turn to the sound of my son's voice. Robby is there with his girlfriend, Serena. Who could even imagine that he's now twenty-one, studying law to work his way up to one day become a judge. He hopes to put away the type of people that once held us prisoners. To say I'm proud of him is an understatement.

I climb to my feet, Enzo too, both of us greeting them, pulling up a chair for each of them, then loading their plates with food that Elena was in charge of preparing.

Elena not only faced her demons and left the center, but she was able to hone her talents in the kitchen, the ones she picked up at Helping Hand, and become a chef. She now has her own restaurant. It's successful enough that she's able to open a new location. I've been proud of her—the girl I once met, and the woman she is today.

"How's school, Robby?" Dante asks. "You're smarter than all of us here. Graduating with honors? I mean, come on." He tosses a hand in the air. "We're all proud of you."

He smiles shyly. "Yeah. Doing what I can."

Serena looks proudly at him, her blonde hair fluttering around her shoulders. They had met in college, studying criminal justice together. She plans to become a lawyer too, but on the defense side. That should be interesting.

When I see Elena cleaning up, I excuse myself and head to her. "Hey!" I call, and she pivots, removing her gloves and throwing them into the trash.

"Jade, hey, I was just getting ready to head out."

"This is for you." I hand her an envelope with a large cash tip.

"You did an amazing job. I'm in awe of your talent."

She looks to me with fondness, her head falling slightly to the side. "It's all thanks to you, Jade."

"No way." I shake my head. "It was all you and—"

"Nah," she cuts me off with a shake of her head. "If it wasn't for your love for us girls, for all the nights you spent on the phone with me, giving me encouragement, listening to me when I was ready to give up, I wouldn't be here."

My heart swells. "I'm glad I managed to do that."

"You remember that last time I called you crying, when I called my mom who said she wanted nothing to do with me unless I had money to give her?"

I nod, recalling that exact moment. My God, she was so broken, she could barely keep herself from hyperventilating.

"Well, if you hadn't gotten in your car and driven up to the center to see me that night, I would've gone back to my pimp. I have a feeling I wouldn't have come back." Tears coat her eyes, but she clears her throat. "I would've ended up dead. I know that's where my life was heading. But you . . . ." Her palm lands across her chest. "You loved us. You helped give us a new life."

My arms circle around her and I hug her to me. "You're an amazing person, Elena. You always have been. You just needed some reminding."

I hear her sniffle as she tightens her own arms around me.

"You deserve to be happy." My mouth widens into a small grin as I pull away. "And I know that with Brandon, that wonderful husband of yours, and those two kids who adore you, you truly are."

"I am." Her sigh is deep and content. "Speaking of kids, I gotta go pick them up from the sitter. It's good to see you guys." She grabs her duffle bag, slinging it over her shoulder. "Come out to eat at the restaurant next weekend. All of you. I'll make whatever you want."

"You spoil us." I grin. "We'll be there. Tell Brandon I said hello and the girls too."

"I will. Tell everyone I said goodbye."

"Take care."

She starts for the gate, and I make my way back, but Elliot stops me.

"You leaving?" I ask him, finding him without Layla, his wife, and Madison, his nine-year-old daughter.

"Nah, just gotta get something for Layla from the car."

"Oh good."

We both smile at one another, and then he marches away, and I do the same. I only make it a few steps before he stops me.

He turns to me just as I twist toward him. "You ever think about our life now and wonder what it would've been like had you not . . ." He trails off, but I know what he wanted to say.

"No." I smile softly. "Because no matter what I went through, everything is how it was meant to be." I walk up to him and place a hand on his arm.

"Yeah, you're right." His gaze zeros in on me in concentration. "I'm glad we got a second chance, Jade." There's much sincerity and love in the cadence of his voice.

"Me too." Emotions riddle through me.

I wish you were here, Mom.

Part IV

MATTEO & AIDA

One

MATTEO
ONE YEAR LATER

A few months ago, we all went to the zoo. Yeah, I know, a bunch of grown men at the zoo. But it was on the bucket list that Enzo had me create a while ago. It's filled with all kinds of things most people in this world have probably done without even thinking twice, but for me, everything is new. Like looking up at the stars, getting licked by a dog, going to the beach, going on a swing. My list would probably look ridiculous to anyone else, but it's mine. All the things I have wanted to experience, but never got the chance. Enzo did help me with it.

So, we took the trip to the zoo, the ladies with us. It was okay.

As okay as it is looking at a bunch of animals living in a cage, thinking they're free. But they're not. Not really. But at least it seemed like they were being well taken care of. But Aida and me, our cage was smaller. The people who hurt us a lot more vicious.

We saw some snakes too, shedding their skin, and I wondered if people can be that way, shedding layers of the rot built on their flesh. Wouldn't that be something? To just excise it all out. Like it was never there at all. To taste, to feel that freedom. That first breath with nothing holding you back.

I'm nothing like the snake though. I still carry the weight of the past, like it never left at all. Will I ever live a normal life? I appear normal, I think. But inside, I'm not. If it weren't for Aida, I wouldn't feel like myself at all. Having her, loving her, it saved me. And it still does.

Our love for one another has only gotten stronger. The bond we formed, the one we share only gets harder to break with each passing day.

We both still have nightmares, and somehow, we ease each other out of them, slowly—whispered words, soft caresses—until we no longer feel the darkness, until it's no longer holding its deathly grip over our hearts.

She convinced me to go to therapy with her months ago—the same woman Jade introduced her to. I can't say she isn't helping, though it took me a while to even talk. I kind of just sat there while she talked instead. She's good at her job because eventually I opened up. We were able to tell her everything we've been through. She's used to people with our past. It's what she does. It was freeing to give my past to another.

But with Aida, I can do anything. I couldn't wait to marry her, and last month, I finally got the chance. My wife. That's another title she now wears, and every time I relive our small wedding on

Corvo Island, not far from the home we built there, overlooking the water, it brings me peace. It was the only thing on my bucket list which mattered—making her my wife.

"You okay?" Dante asks as we ride in the back of Dom's SUV, heading to Dad's grave.

"Yeah, I'm cool." I jerk my chin up to him and he nods, accepting my answer. Enzo is here too, texting, probably with Jade. It's nice to see each one of my brothers happy.

Some time ago, Dom purchased a plot in the same cemetery Mom is buried in. We may not have Dad's body, but we could pretend. We needed somewhere we could go and visit. People need that—a way to connect to the ones we lost. It gives us closure, and none of us ever had that.

And me, I'm still trying. I see him on his knees in that warehouse like it's happening all over again. Maybe one day these images will be more tolerable, less painful. But for now, I hold on to them. I'll never forgive Agnelo and the Bianchis for everything they put our family through. It's not something I'm capable of. But I could figure out a way to move on at the same time.

After the car stops, we hop out, each of us with a bouquet of fresh flowers for Mom—all different kinds and different colors.

It's unfair that my parents weren't buried together. They never bought plots beside each other, so there was nothing we could do about it, but they're close enough.

"Hey, Ma," Dante says, kissing his palm, then placing it against the gray headstone. We each say a few words, placing the flowers there, taking a few private moments alone to talk.

"I miss you, Mom," I tell her when it's my turn. "I wish you could meet Aida. You'd love her."

In this moment, I look up at the sky, taking a long breath, and it's as though I could see her if I look hard enough, there, above the clouds, looking down at us.

AIDA

The girls talk among themselves in the café, but I'm barely listening. Smiling at the right times, my mind drifts toward the past at the oddest moments. Like when I see a man walk in who resembles one of Agnelo's men or when I hear a man's voice and it sounds like one of the ones who hurt me. It's like a string pulling me in, summoning me to the ugliness still embedded within.

It may have been a year, and I thought a year was a long time to get over it. That I'd find solace and healing by now. But I haven't. Not really.

Everything takes time. That's what my therapist likes to say.

Don't rush it, Aida. Everything takes time.

But I'm impatient, I guess. I want to be okay. I want to be normal. Just a girl sitting in a coffeeshop, not thinking about ugly things.

Picking up my cappuccino, I sip, and I sip, and I sip some more, hoping to push down the past. But the pain? The reminders? They still wade up my throat.

I don't know how long it took me to accept that we were safe. That the life we once only imagined is ours now. That he is mine and no one will take him away from me.

Being his wife, it brought on another layer of safety, like an invisible veil, protecting me. I know in reality it means nothing. We can still get hurt, be killed. But he's my husband and I'm his wife, and that's more than we thought we'd one day have.

Everything takes time, Aida.

I'll get there. I'll heal, together with the boy who always loved me, with the man who never gave up.

Helping Hand, the center Jade started, has been a place I find myself going to every week. Not just for the therapy, but for the women who are just like me. Our paths may have been different, but we're all the same in more ways than we'd like to be.

I hear their stories in group, see the tears they shed, the bruises that will take time to heal. Because it does take time. I have to repeat that to myself like a mantra. Don't rush it. One day at a time.

I've come a long way since the beginning, since that very first session when all I did was stare at the wall, hoping it would speak for me. Because how could I tell a stranger everything I went through? The things the man who I thought was my father made me endure. It was difficult. And when I didn't talk, I cried. I cried so much, it became normal. Once the tears purged my soul, I began to speak, until the words fell out of me like the tears once did.

There's freedom in giving that hurt to someone else. It felt like I was cutting it out and handing it to her in my trembling palm. I still felt the bruises on my flesh but I no longer carried the burden. And gradually, I gave her more and more, until I barely had any of it.

"Where shall we do damage next? The Jimmy Choo store?" Chiara asks, drinking her iced coffee while we take a break between stores. It was her treat. She's a giver. I think it makes her feel that she's doing something for us.

"As long as I can pick my feet up and sit my preggo behind somewhere, I don't care," Raquel says, a hand on her stomach. She's due in three months and her feet have just started to swell, but she insisted on coming with us.

"We'll sit you down on the sofa they got there and bring you a virgin drink of some kind," Chiara adds.

"You okay, Aida?" Jade asks quietly, leaning into my side while Chiara and Raquel continue talking.

I turn to her, to the warmth in her eyes and I sigh. "I will be." My lips turn up at the corners. "Everything takes time."

"Yeah, it does," she whispers, wrapping her arm around me and pulling me close. "We just have to get there."

MATTEO

"**D**amn!" Dante whispers from behind me, staring at the paintings I've created of our family.

I had promised to paint each of them something, and I've been working on the artwork for a while. And today, while Aida is with her father, I decided to show them what I've made.

It's crazy to believe that not only do I have my own home, but that my brothers are in it. I got so used to the basement, it was home to me, as fucked up as that sounds. But this place, with Aida, it's home because she's here and we're happy.

"He's like fucking Picasso, man," Enzo adds, bewilderment laced in his tone. "Like legit, you're good, bro. You should have your own gallery. Those rich folks would eat this shit up."

I eye him from over my shoulder, arching a brow. "No." I shrug it off. "Who the hell would want art by a nobody?"

"Every somebody was once a nobody. And you"—he claps me hard around my shoulder—"you're far from a nobody. You're a damn Cavaleri. And our name means something in this city."

I let out a calming breath. "I wouldn't even know how to make that happen."

"Do you want it?" Dom asks, his eyes trapped with sincerity. "Just say the word and we'll make it happen."

I turn to face the multitude of colors, together forming the faces of my parents, my brothers and me too. We're at the bakery in this one. It was an old photo; one we were all in together.

Could I really have my own place? To paint, to sketch what I want and make money for it? My own money?

Maybe. I do know I don't want to run the business with my brothers. They already know that. It's not for me. But Dom still insisted my name be added to the board of their nightclub chain, but I don't actively participate.

This is what I love to do. Watching as a blank canvas comes to life. That's what I love. Painting and drawing, it's my therapy. It's how I get through the reminders of the life before. I become one with it—my mind going elsewhere, while my hands do the work.

"So what do you say?" Enzo asks. "You want to be some fancy-ass artist or what?"

I let out a chuckle. "Yeah, I think I do." I nod.

"Good." Dom takes out his cell and starts typing. "I'll have my secretary look for possible spaces. Give me a few days."

"I'm not in a rush. I've learned to be patient."

I return to my art, staring at all four pieces—one for Aida and me as well. I had each of my brothers go through the photos we got from Mrs. Cuzamano and pick their favorite so that I could replicate it for them.

Finding those photos, it has given us something we never thought we'd get back—a piece of the past. Something we can hold on to, even while so much has been ripped away.

"Incredible." Dante practically chokes up, tracing a finger over Mom's face. We were at the carnival, my mouth smeared with chocolate. I wish I had remembered that day, but I was too little.

"Thanks," I tell him, my eyes going to the one I created for myself. It's a simple one. My parents on the sofa, my brothers and me fooling around on the floor right at their feet, none of us looking at the camera. But Mom and Dad didn't care. They were staring at each other with so much love, I could feel it. And I knew instantly, I wanted that kind of love in my house forever.

AIDA

"How's Matteo doing?" Dad asks, passing some of the mashed potatoes Emma, his wife, had made for dinner. "Why didn't he come with you?"

"He wanted to"—I grab a platter filled with roast beef and add it to my plate—"but he had to do something with his brothers."

"Well, you make sure you tell that fine boy I asked about him, okay?" My father's grin is wide when he talks about my husband and it makes my heart swell, knowing the two most important men in my life get along so well.

"I will, Dad."

I finally take a bite of the food. "The roast beef is wonderful, Emma." I give her a smile.

"Thank you." Her mouth thins and her face lights up. Her attention then wanders to Noah. "Use a napkin, not your sleeve, please," she quietly scolds my half brother. He rolls his eyes at me with a small grin while I let out a quiet laugh.

"I saw that," Emma teases us, shaking her head, her eyes gleaming with joy. I can see why my dad married her. She's kind, a genuinely good person. She welcomed me into her family like it was nothing.

My father and I missed out on a lot. All the memories we could've made. But I won't take the present for granted. It's what we have. And if we don't stop and appreciate it, we'll miss out on living. Because nothing is guaranteed—not the seconds, not the minutes, and definitely not the days.

Once dinner is over, I help them clean up, washing dishes as Noah dries them. Emma brings out chocolate cake while Dad places a freshly made apple pie on the table.

Drying my hands, I get set to join them but, on the way, I stop in the hallway filled with photos of them. Except now, there are photos of me and Matteo too. Some are from the wedding, some from the ones we took during our honeymoon on the island. But my favorite one is of Dad and me, him walking me down the aisle, stopping right before I meet Matteo. His hands, they hold my face, tears in his eyes as he gazes at me. My palm rests over the center of my chest. I feel those emotions as though they're happening all over again.

"I love that one too." Dad suddenly appears.

Wiping a tear from under my eye, I look to him, the kindness sprinkled all over his face. What would my life be like if we hadn't been kidnapped? If I grew up being raised by a man such as him? I'll never know that, but yet I dream of it. I close my eyes and I imagine it all, and it hits me in this moment. The aching of my soul. My heart as though sliced open. It should've been me in this house with him and Mom. We should've had a life together.

"Oh, Daddy," I cry, flinging my arms around him as I let the pain take me away. I find comfort within the arms of a man I never got to love, loving him now, in these fleeting moments.

Three

MATTEO
TWO YEARS LATER

She lies in my lap, her head tucked over my thighs as she stares up at me in our little paradise. We've spent many days on this island, no longer dreaming it, but living it instead.

I place a palm over her growing stomach, our daughter inside. Only a few months until we get to meet her.

Our baby, she will be loved. She will be protected. I can't wait to be a father. I will live my life for her. I will ensure she only sees the good parts of this world as long as I can.

I don't ever want her to find out what happened to her mother and me. Cruelty like that isn't for children. There's already too much broken in the world. I don't want to burden her with our story, or more like our hell.

I know Aida worries about that—if she were to find out. She's afraid of what she'll think, but I'd like to think she'll realize how strong her parents truly are.

"Are we going fishing later?" Aida asks, lifting her hand up, cupping the stubble riding up my jaw.

"If that's what you want, we can. We can do anything, baby."

She sighs, her lips twining up at me and my heart beats for her. "The world, it smells beautiful, doesn't it?" She inhales, her lashes fluttering to a close.

"Nothing is as beautiful as you." I bend my face to hers, our lips meeting in quiet passion.

She leans deeper, angling her face, and I feel it, that love we share. It's everywhere. In the sun. In the sky. In the song that the birds sing high above.

It's a wonder where one can find love when they look for it. And in Aida, I find it all.

AIDA
FOUR MONTHS LATER

How can someone be so small? I stare into my daughter's face, Cecilia Alison Cavaleri. She was born a few days ago at only six pounds and nineteen inches. A tiny doll with the puffiest cheeks we can't seem to stop kissing.

Our living room is filled with voices, all of them wanting turns to hold the newest member of the family. I get up, placing her in my father's arms as his eyes gleam with tears.

"I'm your grandpa, kiddo." He blinks rapidly, unable to hold back his emotions. "She looks like you when you were born, sweetheart." He chokes up. "You had the same cheeks, and you were just as tiny." He laughs, our eyes meeting. "I was afraid to hold you. That's how small you were."

I take a seat beside him, my head on his shoulder as we stare at her, a family, all of us in this room.

She starts to fall asleep, and he hands her back to me, kissing her little foot. I give her to Chiara next, and after that, everyone else gets a chance with her. She has so many people who love her. Who would die for her. She's lucky that way. My beautiful girl. If only Mom and Alison were here to meet her.

Alison.

My throat throbs at the thought of her. I miss her so much, and every chance I get, I visit the makeshift grave we made for her. I needed somewhere to say goodbye, and so did her family. So we decided to give her a proper funeral, with everyone who's ever loved her.

We did the same for Mom too. The two women who were both mothers to the girl and the woman I became. Without them, would I be who I am? I don't believe I would be.

Matteo's still haunted by what he had to do to save me. Shooting her wasn't easy for him, but I had forgiven him long ago. We've all done things we can't take back. It was our life, and we did the best we could.

But our life is better now. I'm studying to become a teacher. Only a year left until I get my degree, and Matteo is happy running his successful gallery in the city. His work hangs everywhere, selling for more money than either of us even know what to do with. I'm proud of him—the boy who'd sketch photos of me.

My God, it feels like forever ago now. I have every single

picture he's ever made me, framed and hanging on the wall of our bedroom, reminding us that love is a simple kind of beautiful.

MATTEO
TEN YEARS LATER - AGE 37

The room's filled with a hum of voices, people scattered all around the gallery I own. The event black-tie and the attendees definitely lived up to the dress code. My brother Dom runs a charity event every year for various organizations, and this time it's for Helping Hand, the nonprofit Jade runs. All the money from my art sold today will be donated to help women just like Aida.

This isn't the first event I've held here. The gallery has grown in popularity in the past years. It's top three in the city and I've sold many of my own sketches and paintings.

Doing something I love, there's nothing like it. And owning

this, having something that's mine, I can't explain it. I never thought I'd ever be here—two kids now, and Aida.

My God, I love her.

She doesn't notice while I stare at her from across the room, a long strappy white gown tight around her curvy body, a modest slit up to her knee. Cyres is in her arms. She's three and prefers her mother hold her still. But Aida, she doesn't mind. She's patient. She's loving. I can't help but fall in love with her more every day that we grow older. She's my muse. My inspiration. She doesn't realize how true that is, even when I constantly remind her.

That long blonde hair flirts across the small of her back, and I have every urge to take her to the back room and rip that damn dress to shreds.

"Fuck," I mutter, running a hand through my hair, not giving a shit that I probably messed it up. "What was that, sir?" Coby, one of my assistants, asks, standing next to me, tapping on the tablet, where he keeps track of the sales.

"Nothing," I say. "Just thinking out loud. But how are you doing? You okay?" I cant my head forward. "Working too hard?"

"I'm doing good, sir."

"How are we doing so far tonight?" I face the two sketches hanging on the wall before me. It's a drawing of two faces merged into one—one part poignant, the other part cheerful. It's about the multidimensionality of humanity. How we aren't just one thing or another.

"Great, sir," he informs. He looks down at the screen, pressing a few keys. "We made two hundred million so far."

"That's great." I nod, knowing how much good that will do for Jade's center.

He goes to make more rounds with the guests, the place large enough to fit one hundred people. Soft music plays in the background, and I just want to grab my wife and dance the night away. We made a life for ourselves, and goddamn it's beautiful.

A ten-year-old Cecilia clutches Dante's hand as they look at a painting I did of her a few years ago, her hair long and blonde like her mother's. It billows in the air, her arms up to the sky as she spins upon the greenest grass, butterflies of all colors dancing with her. The clouds are dark, the storm coming in. But she's dancing anyway, because sometimes that's what we have to do to make it through the darkness.

"Someone bought that one," I tell my daughter, and as she winds toward me, I swoop lower to kiss her on the forehead.

"How could they not?" Dante asks with awe in his voice.

"Thanks," I say, pushing away the compliment. It's never been my thing. I just do what I do, hoping it brings something meaningful to someone else.

"I wish I could paint as well as you, Daddy." Cecilia sighs.

"And I wish I could dance as well as you, angel." She is some dancer. Her ballet teacher says she can try out for one of the top dance schools in the city.

"Sir." Coby walks up to us just then, his thick black brows practically sweating. "There's a woman there who'd like to speak to you about two of your paintings."

"Who?" When he points, my attention wanders to a tall woman, not much older than me, her eyes on the black roses with a green serpent among them. "What's her name?" I ask.

"Stella Emmon."

"Emmon?" Dante's brows rise. "As in Emmon Corp? The dress designer?" His stare widens. "She's rich as hell."

It's then I find Aida, strolling up to her, dropping Cyres who goes to one of my assistants. Aida probably recognized the woman. I know nothing about fashion or business. I let Aida help me with that when she's not busy teaching elementary kids.

They get to talking. Aida's radiant smile has the woman laughing at something she said. I start toward them, steps away, until I'm right behind her. I kiss the back of her head, deeply inhaling her floral perfume, my arm circling around to her front.

"Hey, darling," she says, turning, greeting me with an infectious smile, her palm falling to my bicep. And when she touches me, even after all these years, it's hard not to let it affect me. My muscle there flexes on instinct and my cock begins to harden.

Fuck, now is not the time.

But after this is over—she's mine.

"Hey, baby." My mouth ticks up at the corner.

She clears her throat, those cheeks flushing crimson. "I'd like you to meet Ms. Emmon. She was just telling me what a huge fan she is of your work."

"Thank you." I politely nod, stretching out a hand for her, and she shakes it, her grip a little too tight, her gaze a little too warm.

I think she's after a lot more than my art. Unfortunately for her, cheating on my wife is not on the table.

"Oh, I most certainly am a fan, Mr. Cavaleri." Her bright red lips thin, her eyes glued to mine. "I've been following your work for many years now and I've been dying to own some of your art for my studios." She pivots toward the painting, Aida and I doing the same. "I mean, this is exquisite. It would look divine in my Soho store, don't you think?"

She glances at me over her shoulder, her hand going to my forearm. "You're a very talented man," she purrs, her long, clearly fake lashes flapping as she angles her body toward me, right around Aida, like she isn't even there.

I courteously maneuver myself so that her hand slips right off me, and I use that same arm to tuck my wife against my side.

"Thank you very much, Ms. Emmon. I'm grateful for you and everyone else who could be here tonight for such a great cause."

This pure attempt at flirting makes me hate her. If this wasn't for charity, I'd throw her out. I have no patience for unprofessionalism. I'm sure she can find someone else to screw tonight. It just won't be me.

"Of course." She waves dismissively with an unattractive giggle. "We must do what we can for the lesser privileged."

The way she said that—it was like she was talking about helping the peasants. How does someone like that look at themselves in the mirror? To think they're so much better than others?

"Please look around and let my assistant, Coby"—I point him out—"know which pieces you'd like to purchase."

She nods, fixing the sheer sleeve of her powder-blue ankle dress. Without a second thought, I take my wife's hand and we march away toward Enzo and Dom, their wives with them as they huddle and chat.

"I think she wanted to fuck you," Aida whispers with a giggle.

"Hmm, did she?" Amusement flits in my voice.

"Oh, please. Like you didn't know."

I grip her wrist and spin her flush against me. I cup her jaw and brush my lips with hers, groaning as she lets a little moan slip.

"It's too bad that I only have eyes for you," I breathe. "You own every single part of me, Aida. And I wouldn't change that for the world."

"So," she whispers, biting on her lower lip as her lips flirt with a tiny smile. "You've never wanted to sleep with another woman?" The words slip softly from her mouth.

"Not ever, baby. Not when I have you. And you?" I pop a brow. "Have you wanted to fuck another man, Aida?" My knuckles brush under her chin and her bedroom eyes greet me.

She throws her arms around my nape. "Why would I ever wanna do that?" She rises a few inches on her low heels and kisses my mouth.

My eyes fall to a languid close as I taste her breath on my tongue. My entire body hums with contentment, with need, and affection. When she parts her lips from mine, it's as though I'm empty, needing them back.

"You've been my best friend for my whole life, Matteo." My palm wraps around the back of her head, my forehead falling to hers. "And you, being my husband, it's something that little girl once only dreamed about. Being with you every day"—she sighs—"in our bed, there's nowhere else I'd want to be."

I clench my jaw. "You make my heart weep with how much I love you." My voice throbs with emotion. "When they're all gone, I'm gonna ask Dom to take the kids."

My thumb brushes against her cheek.

"Why's that?" she breathes, backing off a fraction, her eyes boring into mine.

"Because I want you out of that dress," I growl under my breath. "In nothing but that diamond necklace and those heels on."

She sucks in a gasping moan. "And what's going to happen then?"

"Then, Mrs. Cavaleri, I'm going to draw you . . ." I let my hand trace from her arm down to her hip where my hand grips her possessively. "And after that, I'm gonna fuck the shit out of you. Does that answer your question?"

"Ahh, yeah . . ." Her breathing gets shallow. "Quite well."

"Good." I smirk, enjoying her discomfort. "Let's go and sell some more paintings so that there's nothing left for them to stay for."

AIDA

We're finally alone, nothing but the music left, resonating with soft notes into the back of the room where we both are. He's locked the door behind him, just in case, even when the gallery has long been closed.

He leans against the door, the tux wrapped tight around the muscular form of his body. He seems to enjoy the gym, while I enjoy watching him enjoy the gym. We have equipment in the basement of our home, and I much prefer watching him work out than doing it myself.

His eyes wander down my body, my nipples beading under the thin material of my dress. The way he looks at me, it's like he's ready to devour me right on this floor.

"Take off your clothes." His voice hums with command and I find it difficult to make my fingers work. "Now, baby." The muscle in his jaw tics as he stares, the guttural cadence of his tone has me aching between my thighs. "Let me see you." His voice gets all raspy and deep-chested and I grow tingly all over, my skin prickling.

I don't know why I'm nervous. He's drawn me before. But not since I had Cyres . . . I like my body, but not enough to take off my clothes while he sees me with the bright lights shining down over me. There are too many imperfections on my skin these days. And having him draw them, it brings me unease.

He must sense it, his brows tugging before he falls a step toward me, then more until he's close enough to catch my cheek in his palm.

"What's wrong, baby?" The tenderness with which he touches me, talks to me . . . it speaks to me, aches through me.

I glance down, not sure how to voice my insecurities.

He says, "You know I think you're gorgeous, right?"

I nod, and when I still don't look at him, he tilts my face up with the back of his hand. "Let me show you just how beautiful you are."

My eyes prickle. My heart pounds in my rib cage, growing far too large to fill the space there. My gaze perches onto his with adoration, and within his, I find carnal desire burning like embers. I could tell he's hard already without even touching him.

He twines his fingers through mine and takes me to the mirror that lines the entire back wall. My pulse picks up, anticipating what he plans to do.

He stands behind me, and I can see him through the mirror just as his hands find the zipper at my back. Gradually he drags it down, those eyes practically undressing me already.

My skin alights with warmth, spreading over my full body as his fingertips brush down my spine, his mouth leaning into the crook of my neck, lips softly meeting my skin.

"Mine," he groans, his hands slipping into the straps as he draws the dress lower, past my breasts. Those eyes meet me again. "All mine," he growls as his palms cup my breasts, his thumbs slowly sweeping around my hardening nipples. Lust swoops through me in a frenzy and all I want is him inside me.

With a low, breathless moan, my head falls back against his chest, and he brings the rest of the dress down, until it pools around my feet.

I step out of it, now only in a lace nude thong. I look at him then, needing to watch what he'll do to me. He fastens our gaze, like two storms colliding. The intensity of his eyes, it has my stomach flipping. His hand runs from in between my breasts, down over my stomach, a finger tracing my very wet slit.

"Go lie back on that sofa and let me draw every perfect inch of you." He practically groans every word. His lips, his teeth grazing from my collarbone to my shoulder.

"Mmm . . ." I sigh, instinctively cupping my breast and massaging. "These stretch marks," I explain, just as he zaps his attention up. "I—I hate them."

He pauses, his hand resting on my lower stomach. "Oh, baby. Do you think I give a shit? Do you think that it somehow makes you less attractive to me?" He spins me around, both hands clasping each side of my throat, palms stroking my lips. "You could be covered in them from head to toe and I'd still get hard for you above any woman in this entire fucking world. Do you hear me? Do you get how much I love you?" He kisses me against my jaw. "How attracted I am to you?" he breathes.

I can't help it . . . tears burn behind my eyes. Even as I gasp, wanting more of what he's doing, it's too much at once. He brushes under my eyes, and with a kiss to my lips, he kneels, dropping to the floor before me.

Staring up at me with awe, his fingers slip into my panties, and he lowers them to the ground, until I'm nothing but bare skin.

With a long, deep inhale, he presses his mouth into my lower stomach, kissing me in the spots I've come to dislike. Over and over, he loves on my skin, showering me with whispered praises.

"So perfect," he groans. "I can't wait to taste you, to make you quiver around my tongue."

"Oh God," I grumble, grabbing a fistful of his hair. His mouth descends lower until his mouth meets my core, and he drapes my leg over his shoulder, sucking on my pussy. His growling sets me off. I could feel myself grow slick, hunger permeating my every cell.

I yank harder and he backs off, a pure animalistic look on his features. He gets back on his feet, curling his fingers around the back of my head and pulling me toward his mouth with a passionate kiss, his tongue harshly parting my mouth, twirling with the tip of mine before he sucks it into his mouth.

"Fuck," he grits as he draws away. Taking my hand, his fingers gripping my wrist, he leads it to his thick cock. "Feel what you do to me, Aida." He presses my palm into his thick cock and I fight to curl my fingers around it, his trousers in the way. "You see how hard I am for you." I rub him up and down, our lips hovering above one another's, our breaths tangled in need. "I can't wait to watch you swallow my cock with that pussy."

My mouth trembles. I need him now. "Matteo . . . please," I plead.

His eyes shut, head falling back with a groan. "Don't you say my name like that. Not when I intend to draw every gorgeous inch of you first."

"Don't you have enough drawings of me already?" I grab the collar of his suit jacket, pulling him in for a hard kiss. His groaning intensifies as our lips meet once more, fingers spilling into my hair, fingertips dipping into my scalp as he angles me closer, tongue twining with mine. With a harsh tug to my hair, he separates us, teeth, mouth nipping at my jaw.

"Not nearly enough," he rasps, sucking on the skin under my chin. "Now, go lie down on the sofa while I get everything ready."

His heavy-lidded gaze flitters down my curves, and when he runs his hand through his hair, a deep exhale leaving his lungs, he marches toward his supplies.

I make my legs cooperate, even as the flaming desire, that shivery feeling, cascades down my body as I lie on top of the black leather sofa, unsure how to position myself.

He rolls his canvas stand over until it's right before me, getting his equipment ready. And once he does, he removes his suit jacket, his large biceps flexing beneath the tight confines of his white button-down. He places the jacket on the back of the chair while his eyes swim with passion and savagery as they find my naked form spread open for him. The beat of my arousal drums through me, my nipples growing more erect the more he stares at them.

"What the hell did I ever do to deserve you?" He loosens his tie with one quick jerk, and my God, it's the sexiest thing I've ever seen. His masculinity only makes the craving inside me build.

I swallow down the butterflies as he moves closer, looming over me as he picks up my wrist and places my arm over my head, placing the other hand on top of my hip.

I bite into my lower lip, the hair on my arms standing up from his warm touch. He notices, his deepened smirk following the path until he looks into my eyes again. "Stay just like that for me."

He palms his cock as he releases a sharp breath. "You're killing me here."

"I promise not to move." My voice is a mix of hoarse desire. "But you better finish fast or . . ." My fingers drift in between my thighs with a devilish grin.

"Woman," he grits, his jaw tensing. "You get that hand off your pussy. It's mine once I'm done."

I do as he says, returning the hand to my hip. He takes a seat, and once his hands move, those eyes now set with deep concentration, like they're committing my body to memory, I watch him work.

There's beauty in the way he brings his artwork to life, like the objects and people in them are really there, alive on his canvas. Breathing and living and feeling, the way we do.

I knew he was gifted from the moment he first drew us. Best

friends forever is what his picture said, and boy, was he right.

My husband, the artist. The gallery owner. The lover. The father. The survivor.

We survived.

We lived our lives free of the clutches of our oppressors. And though the past is a part of our future, it isn't infinite. It doesn't define us or break us. Instead it makes us stronger. Gives us a brand-new understanding to the world we've been born into.

And there is something special about being with someone who can relate to your pain. I never had to explain myself to him when I was having a particularly difficult day. He understood. He was there. He didn't have to tell me it was going to be okay. He knew I didn't need that. He gave me what I truly needed—a partner who held my hand and let me cry. Let me spill my heart just so he could hold it and nurture it. And over the years, I've done the same for him. We healed each other in many ways. Self-love and therapy.

"Almost done," he says gruffly, his eyes jolting between me and the painting.

"Does that mean we can play now?"

"Oh, we'll play." His smirk lights up his face as he places his brush down, his shirt now splattered with black and red paint.

"You're a little dirty," I say, popping a brow, my bottom lip swallowed up into my mouth as he gets to his feet.

"Then I guess you're gonna clean me up, aren't you?"

Did the temperature in the room just climb up? I let out a sharp exhale.

He puts himself next to my feet, and before I could get up, he grabs one of my ankles, then the other and spins me until my backside hangs off the couch. He lowers to the floor, placing my thighs over his shoulders.

"I've been waiting all fucking night to taste you."

When he tucks his face into my core, his nose brushing in between my slit, my hips shudder, my hands finding the back of his head, writhing beneath him.

"Matteo," I gasp when the tip of his tongue flicks my throbbing clit. He runs circles around it, our eyes meeting in chaotic bouts of pleasure. My body warms. "I need you so badly, I'm willing to get on my knees and beg."

He growls against me as his mouth fastens around my clit, brushing his tongue on me at the same time, while two fingers stretch me wide. My hands tremble as they form fists and I scream out in sweet pleasure, the release ebbing closer.

Suddenly he stops, kissing my inner thighs, too close to where I need him.

"Matteo, please . . ."

"Please what?" His lips land in that space where my leg meets my core, tongue dancing languidly, those dark brown eyes, staring hard. "Tell me what you need? I want to hear every filthy word."

"I need more. I need to come."

"Fuck, I love hearing you say that. Love watching you as you do, knowing I'm the one who gave it to you."

Two fingers run past both sides of my clit and that double sensation causes my eyes to roll back, my back arching, his name like an offering across my lips.

"Yes, don't stop," I pant, scratching his scalp, shoving him back down on my pussy, and the vibrations of his laughter, has me on the cusp. Two fingers sink inside me, the same ones he was using before, and he fucks me with punishing strokes, his tongue ruthless as it brings me pleasure.

"Yes, oh God . . ." My ass grinds on the sofa, my body an electric tangle of nerves. And the final time his fingers thrust deeper, I scream out his name, loud and unabashed.

He does this to me. Every time. He's learned a lot about what brings me pleasure over the years, and I did too. We've spent endless days learning each other. And this man could set me off, merely from a touch of his mouth against the crook of my neck. When the kids aren't around, he fucks me bent over the kitchen counter, snapping my head back by my throat, giving me all the dirty words I crave.

"You're incredible, Aida." His fingers run through my slickness, his eyes feasting on my most intimate place. "So beautiful. Far more beautiful than the stars filling the sky."

I breathe heavy, unable to speak, my body still riding the high, and in a flash, he lifts me off the sofa and into his arms.

"I'm not quite done with you, yet." His eyes hold mine, my legs wrapped around his hips, as he settles himself onto the sofa, me on top. I straddle him as I drink him in, my palm coming to rest on the stubbles of his cheek.

His chest rises, that face filling with a sense of peace and adoration. I finger the buttons of his shirt, and slowly I undress him, needing that connection, wanting my husband inside me. He pulls the sleeves off, those eyes never leaving mine, and I throw the shirt onto the floor.

My hands move to the button of his pants, rolling the zipper down as he watches, palms on the top of my thighs.

His cock jerks. I feel it straining in my hand as I touch it, rubbing in tempered strokes.

He rises, quickly placing me on my feet so he could take off his pants and boxers, throwing them across the room. His cock is all hard. Thick. I touch it. Rolling a fist up and down his shaft.

My walls clench, needing him to fill the emptiness.

"I need to fuck you," he rasps, teeth nipping my bottom lip, his arm circling around the small of my back as he settles me down onto the sofa, taking me with him. "I need to feel what you do to me every time I make love to you." He takes himself in his palm and lines the tip against my entrance. "I'll love you always, Aida. I'll love you until the stars fade and the moon no longer shines. Until we're nothing but dust drifting in the wind. And even then, we'll be together, Aida"—he grabs my hips, his gaze boring into mine—"because my love for you is endless."

"For eternity, then?" I breathe just inches inside me.

"For eternity." Then he slams all the way in, until I'm impaled around him, our heavy groans filling the room.

My mouth greets his once more, my hips rocking against him, stretched and filled to capacity.

"Harder," I cry. "Harder, please."

With a growl, he takes over, flipping me around, positioning my body so he could fuck me from behind.

I hold on to the back of the sofa, his chest meeting my flesh, as he fits the crown of his cock inside me and slams hard until I scream.

His merciless strokes show no mercy, my hair in his clutches as he gives it to me just how I need it.

"I like how wet you get for me," he groans against my ear. "Love you sucking my cock with that pussy, like you can't get enough of it."

"Matteo . . . oh God."

"That's it, baby," he hisses, biting my lobe. "Take it. Every inch is yours." His warm, intoxicating breath flitters against the pulse beating in my neck.

His dirty talk, it sets me off, and I push my ass back, and he smacks it hard. "Dirty girl," he says, doing it again. His hand goes around to fondle my clit, driving me wild. I could feel myself coming undone, just a little more is all I need. But instead of bringing me to orgasm, he takes those fingers and forces them into my ass, playing with me there, sinking inside that hole. And the more he does, the faster his hips pound into, my need almost at the peak.

I find it harder to hold on. Another finger stretches my ass, his cock buried deeper, stroking harder.

"Matteo!" I scream, drowning in intense pleasure.

He works me faster, thrusting deeper, chasing his own release, he pulls my head back, fucking me so hard I almost rip the leather with my long fingernails digging into it.

"Fuuuck!" he growls as he shoots inside me, filling me as he pumps every drop. Once, twice, I lose count, until he stills, falling over my back, his sweat coating my skin, breathing heavy against my nape. "I say we stay here and fuck all night. Let my brother deal with the kids until tomorrow."

I sigh on a laugh. "That sounds tempting. But you know Cyres will wake up crying, wanting her own bed."

"Damn it. You're right." He kisses my shoulder blade, not making a move to get off. I'm okay with that. "I can help you get dressed, then we can go."

"I think I can manage," I toss with a lazy smile.

"I know. But I like dressing you just as much as I like undressing you."

"Is that right?" I breathe.

"Mmm, yeah." He moves a piece of my hair away from my cheek and tilts my face to him with his knuckles. "'Cause it makes me picture you naked all over again."

Heat blooms at my center. A smile turns my lips upward.

When we're this way, loving each other in our own quiet way, I wish I could go back and tell those two little kids in the basement that one day they'll have it all. Once day no one will stop them.

They'll love each other out in the open, and every day, they'll be further away from the horrors of before.

Five

AIDA
THIRTY YEARS LATER - AGE 67

Dear Diary,

It's been a while since I've written. A good fifty years in fact. Sometimes I read the things I had written to you when I was there, in that house, with that monster of a man, and I can't believe that was me. Because my life, it's been good. So good. For those first few years, I feared it was a mere illusion, casting me in a spell. But it's real—my life, the love we found.

Matteo and I, we have each other, our children, our sweet grandchildren, and we treat every day like it's a gift.

We made up for everything we had lost, everything we had missed out on. We even crossed off everything on Matteo's bucket list, including skinny-dipping. Boy, was that fun.

We tried that again a time or two. But these days, my old bones can't take much *of that. I'll always have the memories though, the days filled with sunsets and laughter, and the beauty of life reborn from the dusk of our despair.*

So, it's time to say goodbye, my old friend. This will be my last entry. You served me well, like a true friend, and I'll never forget you.

I close the diary, the same one I had since I was fourteen, the one Alison had given me for my birthday, and I place it on top of my lap.

"What are you writing, sweetheart?" Matteo drapes an arm around me, pulling me in for a kiss.

"Just how much I love you." I drop my head over his shoulder and his lips touch the top of my head.

"Not as much as I love you." He sighs as we swing a gaze at our six grandchildren, making way too much noise, but we don't care because that's how it's supposed to be. That's what I always wanted.

His laughter rumbles from beside me as he watches Sasha, the three-year-old, wrestle her cousin Mica. "I hope I've given you everything you dreamed of," he says with affection tethered to his voice.

"Everything and more, my love. Everything and more."

The End

Playlist

- "Smoke" by Bobi Andonov
- "Blood on Your Hands" by Veda feat. Adam Arcadia
- "Lose My Breath" by Rhea Robertson
- "Better" by Emma Remelle
- "Morning" by Goldilox
- "Love Made Me Do It" by Ellise
- "Everything" by SMNM
- "Wake Me Up" by Tommee Profitt feat. Fleurie
- "Sensitive Little Razorblade" by Perish
- "Come Away With Me" by Norah Jones
- "Remembrance" by Tommee Profitt feat. Fleurie
- "Arise Like Fire" by Jonathan Buchanan feat. Michael Lister
- "Middle Finger" by Bohnes
- "When It's All Over" by Raign
- "Monsters" by Ruelle
- "Home Again" by UNSECRET feat. Aron Wright
- "Never Stay Down" by UNSECRET feat. Sam Tinnesz
- "Fearless" by UNSECRET feat. Ruby Amanfu
- "The Reckoning" by UNSECRET feat. Matthew Perryman Jones
- "Gotta Love It" by Ruelle
- "It's You" by Jesse Villa feat. Mikey Geiger
- "Journey (Ready to Fly)" by Natasha Blume

- "Can't Knock Me Down" by Pretty Panther feat. Anna Mae
- "This Is the Beginning" by Ely Eira

Also By Lilian Harris

Fragile Hearts Series

1. *Fragile Scars* (Damian & Lilah)
2. *Fragile Lies* (Jax & Lexi Part 1)
3. *Fragile Truths* (Jax & Lexi Part 2)
4. *Fragile Pieces* (Gabe & Mia)

Cavaleri Brothers Series

1. *The Devil's Deal* (Dominic & Chiara)
2. *The Devil's Pawn* (Dante & Raquel)
3. *The Devil's Secret* (Enzo & Jade)
4. *The Devil's Den* (Matteo & Aida)
5. *The Devil's Demise* (Extended Epilogue)

Messina Crime Family Series

1. *Sinful Vows* (Michael & Elsie)
2. *Cruel Lies* (Raph & Nicolette)
3. *Twisted Promises* (Gio & Iseult)
4. *Savage Wounds* (Adriel & Kayla)

Savage Kings Series

1. *Ruthless Savage* (Devlin & Eriu)
2. *Brutal Savage* (Tynan & Elara - September 6th, 2024)
3. *Wicked Savage* (Fionn - January 6th, 2025)
4. *Filthy Savage* (Cillian - May 5th, 2025)

Standalone

1. *Shattered Secrets* (Husdon & Hadleigh)

For Lilian, a love of writing began with a love of books. From *Goosebumps* to romance novels with sexy men on the cover, she loved them all. It's no surprise that at the age of eight she started writing poetry and lyrics and hasn't stopped writing since.

She was born in Azerbaijan, and currently resides in Long Island, N.Y. with her husband, three kids, and a dog named Gatorade. Even though she has a law degree, she isn't currently practicing. When she isn't writing or reading, Lilian is baking or cooking up a storm. And once the kids are in bed, there's usually a glass of red in her hand. Can't just survive on coffee alone!

Lilian would love to connect with you!
Email: lilanharrisauthor@gmail.com
Website: www.lilanharris.com
Newsletter: https://bit.ly/LilianHarrisNewsletter
Signed Paperbacks: https://bit.ly/LHSignedPB
Facebook: www.facebook.com/LilianHarrisBooks
Reader Group: www.facebook.com/groups/lilianslovlies
Instagram: www.instagram.com/lilianharrisauthor
TikTok: www.tiktok.com/@lilianharrisauthor
Twitter: www.twitter.com/authorlilian
Goodreads: https://bit.ly/LilianHarrisGR
Amazon: www.amazon.com/author/lilianharris